D0710312

IN BROKEN WIGWAG

IN BROKEN WIGWAG

by

Suchi Asano

Rosset-Morgan
A Division of United Publishers Group

Rosset-Morgan
A Division of United Publishers Group Inc.
50 Washington Street
Norwalk, Ct. 06854

ISBN: 0-8038-9399-X

Library of Congress Catalog Card Number: 97-071277

Printed in the United States of America

10 9 8 7 6 5 4 3 2 1

for J.O.

I wish I was a photographer. I wish I was a someone who can convey emotions in visible form.

I wish. I wish. I wish—way back when this 'wish' has became my pet monkey. I'd take it out my pocket at times till I had enough and put it back again. I'd cuddle and caress it whenever I need some heart's ease.

Here is a photo sitting on my desk in front of me. Taken probably in the thirties, in an Indiana farmtown main street. A photo of a girl holding a man's—perhaps her father's—hand in the crowd. She looks a bit nervous. Perhaps she is a farm girl who isn't used to the crowd of people, or she maybe on her way to a small town talent contest to sing in the public for the first time in her life. (She has a pretty gingham dress on.)

You can't be quite sure of what the circumstance is. But you can see her trust in the man whose hand she's holding. Though her face reveals the anxiety, her arm is loose, relaxed, as if the arm has a life of its own. She is ready to be taken to wherever the man will take her, to a barber, slaughterhouse, even Grandma's death bed, as long as her hand is closed in his firm hand.

You can tell that.

Sometimes I wish I could express my emotion by means of color and texture. Sadness would be in the blue hue—the deeper the sadness, more greyish the blue gets.

Anger could be in deep lurid red, varies in thickness, almost watercolor-like tenuity to muddy, tar-like consistency. Overjoy is in gold. Just like the way summer sky gets after a late afternoon shower. Very Sistine Chapel.

But in reality, needless to say, when I want to let people know my feelings I have to deal with words. Words is the currency of emotional exchange, whether you like it or not. I'd try to pay my best effort, but it always leaves me depressed, discouraged.

With words, I barely seem to trace my feelings. It's like a 3-D print. When what I want to express is supposed to be in red shape, what comes out is always a little off—same shape but in green. And I don't have special glasses to overlap them in one.

It doesn't seem to matter which language I speak. Of course, with English it occurs much more often, but it still happens with my native tongue of Japanese nonetheless. I'd try carefully to sort out all the words to choose from in my head, but what comes out of my mouth is not always what I mean to say. I can get it close, but that's all it gets.

Close. Approximation. The bits I couldn't form into words trickle down drop by drop and remain collected forever like a stalactite.

What's worse, while I'm hung up with elaborating the words, I begin to wonder if my emotion is genuine. I can't help wondering if I'm tailoring my emotion to fit to the readily words that have been lying around.

Am I a hand in a borrowed glove or am I a glove adapted by a hand?

1

"Take anywhichone you want, O.K.?" Kira says, and hurries toward the kitchen area, still wearing shades and a wide-brimmed hat.

Behind her, late afternoon sun stretches lazily over a panoramic view of SoHo rooftops. Watertowers and roof gardens, it's another world that you can't guess from the street. It stuns me every time I see it.

"O.K., well, let's see . . . " I say as I sit down on the edge of the small boat-like king size bed.

In front of me are four garbage bags full of clothes, which Kira mentioned over the phone. She told me she's been cleaning up her closet, and wanted know if I would like to take some of unwanted home before the disposal. I told her for sure. Why not, indeed.

"Still, there are so much to look through! Are you really gonna throw all this away?" I ask her when she comes back from the kitchen.

"Not *throw*ing away, *giving* away, to Salvation Army. There's no point to clutter your life with unwanted stuff—don't you think?"

She hands me a cranberry juice.

"Hmm. . . ., I suppose so. Thanks."

Still, is there any way she can get rid of these stuff and make a profit?

I take a sip from the ruby-red liquid, and wonder if it's a ill-bred of me to put down the glass on the floor.

I'm not sure about what the proper etiquette is. Not that it matters much if I prove my lower-middle upbringing. Well, maybe a little.

I hesitated a moment, then put the glass down on the dresser, right next to the latest issue of Italian Vogue.

"O.K., let's get to work."

Rubbing hands like a thief yet to open newly acquired coffer, I dig in. It could be an off-season Christmas for me. Kira is a connoisseur of clothing, needless to say.

I start to fish out the garments one by one.

First piece—a pair of black leggins with rose print—too faded. Out, I say. Second, is a striped Indian shirt—looks new, but too flimsy. Not my cup of tea. Next one is a truly wrinkled but still ultra-stiff second-hand blazer—this could send off Armani to a dermatologist for hive break out. Then, again, a faded mid-riff top. . . .

What's all this about? Where have they been hiding? Whatever happened to her Dolce & Gabbana or J.P.G.? The Christmas baloon is losing air rapidly . . .

"I know they look like they come from the bargain bins outside Canal Jean," Kira kids, giggling nervously, obviously sensing my disillusion.

"But some of them should be in a pretty good shape, I swear."

The instant she says that, the conversation we had a little while ago comes back to my mind.

* * *

It was late May, and the temperature was already shooting up to nineties despite the ice age winter that preceded it. "The second highest in the recorded history" the weatherman stressed. It's funny when an unusually cold weather strikes, we talk about return of ice-age, and unusually warm or hot weather visits on, we zero in on ozon layer.

Kira and I were chatting in a cafe where a ceiling fan was circling in full speed to shake off the rust left by the hard frost.

We were complaining this and that to each other as usual, just like girls do. In a course of conversation we started talking about the weather which had turned from one extreme to another. I told Kira that if summer came this early, I wouldn't have anything to wear. All of my summer clothes were beat from excessive laundring, and that I couldn't afford summer clothes. I'd just moved into a new apartment.

As far as I remember, I didn't make it sound too pathetic; my remark on not having clothes came by, as a matter of fact, as a conversational flow. I didn't mean much, well, even if I meant it, I was and am always pretty careful about not to appear too concerned.

But now, I've begun to feel that Kira has decided to show some mercy on me; playing a philanthropist. For me—poor Satomi, who lives in a dingy little cubicle in Far-East Village.

When Kira came over to my new place for the first time, I didn't miss an expression of horror overtook her face.

As I opened the door to let her in, she just stood there,

with her usual it's-showtime-folks-smile stuck halfway, which reminded me of a ventriloquist's dummy. She looked a bit out of place even with her most pared down outfit—an army fatigue parka and jeans. Her make-up a little too precise; her hair too neat in place. Everything was too calculated to look *down*.

After a couple of beat she seemed have made up her mind to risk her health. (Perhaps she was worried about the possible contamination of rat-dung-disease.) She handed me a bouquet of pink peonies as a house-warming present. Just then I realized that was what made her look peculiar—nothing looked more odd in this place than bountiful flowers.

She muttered a few words quickly—"it's so cozy" or something—or I thought she did. I could tell she was utterly at a loss for words. It must have been shocking to her, but it was also shocking to me to receive an affirmation of my desolation: this place was, in anybody's eyes, as shitty as I'd suspected.

I know she was trying the best she could. To find some nice thing to say, to be positive. I know.

" Hey, Mac! C'me 'ere."

Kira's cat, Macintosh, plops down on the clothing pile I've been creating.

" Come here, I say."

Kira grabs him up (or more like peels him off), from the red mariachi shirt he is ready to mush.

" Macky, Macky-Mac, Macki-di, Macki-de, koo—"

Kira rocks him in her arm with a baby-talk. I smile. The scene makes me feel like having a cat too.

"By the way, what became of your possible showing in a gallery?"

I venture out the question I've been dying to ask ever since I got here. I feel my blood pounding faster than usual under my chest.

"Oh, that . . . " She keeps stroking the cat.

"They say I need at least ten large pieces, which means, with the size of the canvas I work with, I need minimum twenty. So that was that."

She shruggs as-a-matter-of-fact-kind of way. She doesn't seem particularly disappointed. I give a sigh of relief. I would have felt somewhat unfair if she had told me she was going to have a show. If her paintings deserve a showing, so do mine. I'm at least as good as she is, I think. Although I, too, haven't done many of them. Yet.

While Kira brushes the cat, I take out a few more garments out of the bag. By this time I know for sure that it was my paranoia to think Kira's doing me a charity. I've gone through two and a half bags so far and haven't found anything one calls a treasure. They are all like the ones you see displayed on the pavement of Third St. and Ave. A, in a hardly traffic-able condition. Kira knows I can afford *them.* (She does, doesn't she?) Perhaps for her attachment to the garments, she couldn't hand them straight over to a complete stranger without blessing. She **loves** her clothes. Dearly. The trouble is that sometimes the love last for a long time, and other times only until she comes home with it in a shopping bag.

"Oh, you gotta try that on!" Kira says, pointing with her chin to the double-breasted jacket that I've been smoothing out.

"It's Stephen's. I picked it up for him, but he doesn't think it's *him*."

"Really? I like pin-stripes myself. Does he think it's too *Borsalino* or something?"

"I don't know. He thinks my choice of clothing a little too theatrical."

We burst out laughing. It's such an understatement. Kira owns a few clothes that make people in the street double-take on her.

"Where's Stephen now?"

Mac wiggles out of Kira's enfolding, having had enough lovee-dovee.

"In Italy or Switzerland, I believe. He's supposed to be home on Thursday . . . Hey, that jacket looks really nice on you."

"You think so? Can I see it in a mirror?"

"Sure. Here."

Kira opens the massive armoire which is packed with clothes still in dry cleaner's plastic bags.

"Hmm. . . ."

The jacket does look pretty good on me. It fits big, but its bignesss seems playful, and its rigidness softens on a girl. But for a guy, particularly for Stephen, whose freckled face reminds me of Midwestern farmland (although he is from Boston area), it could look too stiff, overdone.

"Well, when he sees me wearing this, he may ask it back, will he not?"

I say, though not quite sure when would I ever see him. He seems to be elsewhere all the time on his buying trips for his objets d'art (I guess that's what you call them) store.

"Don't worry about what *he*'ll say. It's yours now."

She says rather bluntly, and takes off the shades and the hat.

"Wow! It's a whole different world!"

She checks herself closely in the mirror. After having been diagnosed as having atopic dermetites, she's been very fussy about hiding herself from the sun. When and if the automated blind of the living room gets stuck (it seems to happen every so often), she goes around the apartment with a hat and shades.

"Say, Satomi, is your sister really coming to New York?" Kira asks at my reflection in the mirror, pulling her eyelid upward.

"Yeah, apparently. In a few weeks time. She is supposed to tell me when she books her flight."

"That's great! We can have fun. We can take her—where can we take her?"

All of a sudden she looks slightly tense.

"The Statue of Liberty, of course."

"No! Really?"

"No. I don't know. Maybe she'd like that. But what she tells me is she wants to enjoy the New York atmosphere more than anything else."

"In other words, she wants to hang around, more or less?"

"Right. She'd like to be a New Yorker for a month."

"Ugh . . . " She makes a wierd sound, then says,

"Sorry. I don't mean your sister, but I can't stand the way they—Japanese magazines and such—completely distort everything! New York: how cool and exciting! It's always this '*kooru de ekisaitingu* ,' like they don't know any other adjectives. They make this place sound so happening even down to buying a toilet paper or emergency Tampax in the middle of the night. And people swallow all that B.S. . You know what I mean? Damn!"

I understand what she means. It's more poignant when you were the one among many who came here inspired tremendously by these traveler's tales. I like it here fine, but at the beginning I had to reconcile myself to take in the place as it traversed before my eyes. I guess that what you call 'facing the reality'.

"You'd definitely need some adjustments between what you were told and what you see. But, don't worry, she's not misguided enough to play a homeless in Shinjuku Chuo Park . . . Well, I hope not!"

At this, she laughs.

"Haven't seen her a while?"

"Three years."

"Wow! That must be exciting for you, too, then. . . .Like, is she a club-kid type?"

"No, I don't think so. She is already twenty-five . . . "

"Oh, c'mon, Satomi, don't say stuff like she's *already* twenty-five. What are we, then? . . . Anyway, that's kind of good. To tell you the truth, I wasn't exactly up to taking her out clubbing night after night. It's a little too—oh, I don't know, I really am getting old." She laughs, a hair forcibly. I think it's funny that she seems to think my sister's having a good time is somewhat her responsibility.

"But, you do go out at night, don't you?"

She tells me the stories of her hang-over once in a while.

". . . Well, yeah, when Stephen's around . . . "

She acknowledges reluctantly. There's a touch of irritation in her voice.

"Listen, shall we talk about where to go to eat?"

2

Having turned on the lights and triple locked the door, I feel all of a sudden drained.

I plonk down on the futon sofa and unlace my shoes. Without releasing my feet free, I can't be truly comfortable. It's very Japanese, I suppose.

"God, I'm tired."

As soon as the words spills out of my mouth, I realize I'm the only listener. I get to the sink, gulp down some water, and look for some Tylenol, but all I find is an empty bottle. I throw it in a trash and let out a sigh.

. . . Although Kira is practically my only friend (it's hard to admit it even to myself but she is), I get weary of her sometimes. I mean, I like her and she's been a good friend to me, but sometimes she goes completely berserk. She seems to be getting bitter and harder—she always had these streaks but they seem to strike up more and more often now. Maybe it's induced by the hormonal imbalance—Actually she may have mentioned something about that in the past, but I don't know for sure.

Today at a Japanese restaurant, she attacked a girl for no reason. No reason at all. This girl was at the wrong place at the wrong time (sorry!), just by out of luck. It wasn't physical, though (or therefore), it was pretty vicious attack.

We were sitting next to a table of four garrulous and excited kids. They seemed to be thrilled about anything and everything down to, most of all, being alive. They were what we call in Japan of the age that even laugh at a tumbling of a chopstick. Two boys, two girls: probably university freshmen, from good suburban families, who during their city living have discovered eating exotic food hip. Except one of the girls was definitely Japanese.

A Westerner may wonder how, but we can pretty much pick out a fellow countryfolk from other Asians; just like an American can spot other Americans in foreign land. It's the same thing. It's not only the accent that make us spottable, but in our case, it's a look: we all seem to have drifting eyes—spawn of too much self-consciousness, maybe. And I'm the worst example of them all.

. . . .To be honest, even the fact that I must use 'I' everytime to discribe *my* conduct, anything *I* put *my* hands on, throws *me* into a fidgety state: Like I'm afraid I may be displaying excessive self-interest. 'I' did this, 'I' do that, I, I, I. . . . I wonder if this perpetual use of singular pronouns since birth contributes to a formation of one's individuality. Unlike Japanese where subject and object are sometimes left to a listener's guess, in English 'I' is so clearly distinguished from others, as if each of 'I' is carefully kept in latex, not to be mixed up with the next 'I'. Is that why Americans are not scared of being unapologetic for standing up for themselves, and I'm only half way there? On the other hand British people(for that matter, Australians and Irish) speak English and they are a lot different from Americans. Hmm . . .

Well, enough of that. Now I'm going back to where I left off—the Japanese girl.

She was a plain-looking girl as far as conventional beauty goes, but she knew how to put together things to work for her, like a lot of other Japanese girls. Obviously young; barely twenty. Her red lips were those of a child trying out her mother's make-up kit. Unthreatening, almost smile-provoking looking.

The conversation was being carried mostly by the other three and the Japanese girl didn't pitch in much but when she did—a few words, slowly—she made her party guffaw, and her face would glow. It was obvious she was having a good time.

As we were finishing up our dinner, I noticed Kira had been eyeing their table sideways. Rather audaciously, particularly at the girl. A cold look of disapproval, like the ones she throws at the people who are wearing loud but three-years-behind-the-trend clothes. Fortunately the girl didn't notice Kira's stare, I thought at first, for she was looking straight at her friends, but then I became certain that she was only pretending not to have noticed. For she never once threw a glance back at us, which was hard to swallow. When somebody stares at you that close you'd notice. The girl must have seen what was going on but had little idea what was all about exactly, decided to shut it out. Sometimes it's best to ignore things. What else could she do otherwise? Would she face Kira and ask her up front, "What are you looking at?" No! If she wasn't a Japanese maybc, but she was, and what's more, she was young and new in the city, there wasn't even a chance in a million she would do that. And Kira was fully aware of it. I tried to surmise what's up with her. It was true that they were noisy enough to make other diners' heads across the room turn around. But what can you do? To silently pressure a girl to tell her party to be quiet?—that wouldn't do. I knew people from the restaurant weren't going to do anything, so only thing we could do was just finish off eating and leave. Which wasn't hard to do since we were almost through anyway.

"—And then he says,' no money, no honey, no funny!'"

"Oh, no!"

Another frantic roar. Kira rolled her eyes deliberately.

I popped the last piece of California roll into my mouth and, though there were a few more pieces left in her plate, asked Kira if we should get a check. I could tell she was quite distracted; having to abandon eating, she was twisting the chopstick wrapper, turning it into look like a primer. I was getting anxious.

"Check? Sure."

A waitress came over to pour some tea, and asked our next table if they wanted anything. It brought them a quiet moment. That's when Kira fired off, setting her eyes directly at the girl.

"WHAT A G-R-E-A-T WAY TO COMMUNICATE, GRINNING LIKE A MORON! HARDLY NEEDS ENGLISH!"

Then she turned to me,

"You know, I just can't believe some people think they can talk to others without knowing a word of English! These people, celebrities, writers, whatever, come to New York, spend two, three months, go back to Japan and tell everybody publicly—since they think whatever they do deserves a public attention—'oh, I made so many friends there, it's like a whole New York is friend of mine, thanks to my happy-go-lucky personalilty!' In the meantime, all they did here was just grinning—So conceited or what!?"

She drew out a quick breath in satisfaction, and gulped down some water. I gave a quick glance at the girl. From the corner of my eye, I could see her being shook up. She was in a blank shock: her smile dangled frozen like she didn't know whether to laugh it off or cry. The ambiguous expression made her look much older. I sensed the gaze emanated from the guy next to her toward us, dubious.

Kira and I walked a couple of blocks in silence until she finally uttered,

"I . . . It was terrible, wasn't it?"

What was I supposed to say?

"I know . . . God, how could I have done that? Why? What got into me?"

I couldn't bear looking at her, so I walked on straight, trying to gain some time till words would return to me.

On Houston Street, retail shops were already shut up, and a few remaining restaurants were taking sidewalk tables inside. One more weekend was coming to a close.

Just about when I was passing by the cafe on the corner

of McDougal where a fat orange cat sleeps on the stool, I realized Kira wasn't with me.

I turned around immediately—(Why did I do that? I could've gone home)—only to find her standing against the fence of basketball court. Now, if I were a man and if it had been drizzling, it could have been a scene from an old French movie: a girl, twenty-eight or thereabout, her long hair disheveled, trench-coat falling loosely from her shoulder, black high-heels, leaning forlornly against unreachable darkness. (. . . Roll the camera . . . Action!)

I clicked the tongue in my heart and went up to her.

"Kira—"

" I don't know—. It's awful. I feel awful."

She shook her head as if trying to sober up.

"Kira, don't—"

"No! I can't take it. I can't let it—"

She buried her face in her hands, broke down sobbing.

I stood there, didn't know what to say or do, fighting off the curious gaze of strollers. For the first time in my life I wished I were a man. By holding and kissing her, to bail her out of tears. But as a girl, I was lost.

She kept sobbing for a while until all of a sudden she raised her face as if she had found an alternative alleviative. Her eyes had a strange, fixiated glare.

"Y'know, I'm going back to the restaurant and apologize her. Yes, that's it. I have to tell her I was a way beside myself . . . But do you think she'll forgive me? Do you? Say she will, please, Satomi . . . "

I let out the longest sigh.

"Listen, Kira. Let's forget about everything, O.K.?

What's done is done. They won't be there. The restaurant is closed. She'll get over—"

I went on, minding not to sound too grim.

"—By tomorrow, she'll be telling her friends about you, like 'I was bullied by this bitch who was insanely jealous of my youth!'."

God, I really don't have a sense of humor.

"Do you think so?" Kira looked up, hopeful and full of coquetry. I gave a swallow.

"Yeah, sure. It's like a metabolism, you know. New cell born, old cell gone. Constant renewal. She'll forget, you'll forget. Only we can't go to the same restaurant again. Waitresses will remember you. But that's not the end of the world, is it?"

I managed a smile.

"Well, . . then. O.K. . . ."

She took out a tissue from her coat pocket and blew her nose.

". . . I'm sorry, Satomi."

"It's all right . . . Are you O.K. now?"

"Uh-huh."

She fingered off the ringed smudges around the eyes and nodded.

We started off again toward Sixth Avenue. The lukewarm stickiness of June air reminded both of us of home. The summer must be starting overthere too, I thought.

While we waited for the light to change, Kira muttered.

"Most people would say they need a vacation, but I'd say I need a work."

And I didn't say anything.

3

Yoshiko is Kira's real name in her passport. It means 'good child' in Chinese characters. It can also be read as 'Ryoko'.

Kira once told me,

"Originally my namc was meant to be Ryoko. But the maid, who was sent down to the resistrar's office to apply for my birth certificate, since my parents couldn't make it there themselves, put 'Yoshiko' in the pronounciation column! Can you believe it!?"

No, I don't think so.

She rarely tells people her real name. She thinks it's dumb.

* * *

Kira doesn't flush toilet to cover up pissing sound. When asked she said,

"It's such a terrible waste of water! Do you have any idea how many gallons of precious water goes down the drain virgin-pure everyday for this silly ritual? What are you afraid of if somebody hears you're pissing? I mean whatelse do you do when you get in a toilet except shit, piss, fuck, and do some dope—give a birth to a baby . . . ? Well, I guess it's possible."

The truth is she thinks it's unbearably Japanese.

*   *   *

Kira's special talent is that she can shed tears at the drop of a hat. For this talent, she appeared in seven different TV commercials before she was a year old, and tricked numerous boys later in her life.

Hmm. . . .

4

A boomy base line of acid jazz is coming from the floor above, with the clonky sound of heels hitting my ceiling. The sign of life, the weekend party. There they go again. . . .

There are three things I can't quite get use to: rice puddings; pissy smell of the street in the summer; and parties. The first two I can either avoid or forget about it quick enough, but parties, man, it's a kind of necessary evil for me. Even if I may come home exausted and heartbroken, I gotta go sometimes so I can be in touch with society or whatever I need to be a part of. Do I really want to be? How desperate am I?—I question sometimes, but I don't want to be the one of those women who have gone disconnected one day and just rant in rags all the time in a park. It really scares me, possibility of falling into that state. So I go out even knowing the outcome beforehand. It generally ends up to be a harsh reality check that I'm so helplessly dull.

I'm not good at standing around in parties. Especially when there's music blasting from the speakers at the dial turned all the way to the right. It makes me uneasy and soon my palms would become sweaty. Then I'd start hear loud hard-knuckled bangs coming through the wall. A complaint from a next door neighbor—a guy in a wife-beater pounding the grease-stained wall with a fist loaded with all the rancors he has against the world. A grudgehammer.

One for what he is, another for what made him the way he is. He'd keep pounding and pounding . . .

I used to listen to lots of music as a teenager. Japan, The Fall, Joy Division. It was a moment of placid tranquility, the time I could be alone without any guilt or pressure.

After the rest of our house had gone to sleep, I'd drop the needle ever so delicately onto the whirling trough of the vinyl and put on the headphones. I loved headphones so much. Not only for their sci-fi look, but for their sending me into an another dimension, so detached from everything else. The space that is so calm and still, and I'm the only thing moving in the whole place—I myself remain lying motionless, but at the same time drift further and further away, into the starry universe that filled with music—Though it resonates sonorously, its reign so absolute it becomes silence. And I'd keep floating away . . . away. . . . .

Then, out of nowhere, my father would come storm into my room, his face still bright pink from the drinks, yell his gut out,

"WHAT TIME DO YOU THINK IT IS!? GO TO SLEEP FOR HEAVEN'S SAKE!"

It scared a hell out of me every time he did this. By invading my room, he invaded my serenity altogether. I hated him for that. He claimed he could hear the noise coming through the floor(through the headphones!). That was because he acutely tuned in to find anything reproachable. He had a sleeping problem.

I know it's not fair to blame him for my shyness. But sometimes I just can't ignore that there's definite resemblance between us, as if cowardice is a hereditary.

I met Kira at the typical New York house party, only this was a rather upscaled one. It was in SoHo, so it was very likely that the place belonged to an artist. It had lofty ceiling, bright track lights, gigantic mirrors, but I don't remember seeing any work in progress. Well, the occupant may have been a miniaturist for all I know. I was more impressed with the waiters agilely zigzagging among the people, holding tall champagne glasses steadily on the tray.

I was there with Kevin, my boyfriend at the time. That makes it four (or five?) years ago. With a steady boyfriend and job, it wasn't a bad period for me.

As usual, apart from trailing Kevin to hover over and peck at the conversation he was having with someone, I had nobody to talk to. There were enough people—must have been twenty, thirty of them there, though not a single soul I could talk to. It's not that I wasn't interested at all: the party had a sort of artistic atmosphere, there were some interesting looking people for sure.

But no. These people are not for me, I thought. I haven't got a clever one-liner to get their attention nor wit to magnetize these people. They haven't got a time for me. I'm not clever, I'm not pretty, I'm not on television. There's nothing extraordinary about me whatsoever. How can I ask them to be interested in and have some patience with me?

When there's music I'd say I can't talk because I can't hear people, and when there's no music, I'd find myself tongue-tied.

To break the ice, I'd need a chainsaw. Besides, it gets me depressed to see someone disconcerted because of me: someone who tries to comprehend at what I say and at the same time hides the fact that they don't understand. Out of politeness they'd do that, I know, and that makes me feel sorry for what I put them through. What's worse is it tends to happen with nicer people. Nice people who try.

Tender betrayal hurts more than spiteful farewell, said who.

Still, I stood around, smoked cigarette after cigarette, in an attempt to look poised. I know it's a cliche to smoke to be cool, but there aren't many alternatives available, are there? Yet.

Sixty seconds became a minute, a minute repeated five times, nothing happened. Some people smiled at me when they passed by me. I smiled back. But it didn't go any further. Maybe they were smiling at something else and I happened to be in a way. I took another drag from the cigarette.

When one of catering girls bumped into me, I lost my composure. I started to feel conspicuous as a llama on a golf course or a red dress at a funeral. I felt like everyone in the room had seen me standing ineptly alone.

I went around the room to look for Kevin. To persuade him to go home. I needed him. I needed him to caress me, hold me. To tell me he loves me as I am, that I'm not such a terrible person as I make out. But he wanted me to wait ten minutes until he finished his business.

"Ten minutes. No more. I promise," he said and winked, using his charm to the full extent.

I felt blank. To my shame, I could feel tears welling up in my eyes.

I just wanted get out of there. Nothing else. Nothing mattered anymore. The door was kept wide open, I dashed toward it. I didn't know if I was going to leave there by myself. I had no idea what I was going to do.

It was when I came out to the hallway, I saw Kira.

Memory is a strange thing. It needs a lot of explanation, the way it works. On the one hand it could be so elusive that you can not retrieve when you want it most desperately. (Just as we all experienced during school years, especially before the exams.) On the other it creeps up on you when you are not ready, or sometimes amazes you by spreading accounts in such a detail of an event you didn't take particular notes on.

I remember what Kira had on that night. It was a white cotton piquet dress with big tulip print, tightly fitted, in which her voluptuous body seemed to be rebeling against the confinement. Her bosom looked like they could burst out in any minute, like some tropical fruits falling from the tree with a thump—the thought reddened me.

It was like stepping into a colored world from murky world of black and white. There was this girl, sitting on the floor with her legs stretched out like a doll, thick black hair, bright red lips that matched the color of tulips which looked tossed around in praise for her vitality.

I caught my breath and blushed, this time with shame for having been such a crybaby.

She perched her intense gaze on my face for a long time as if she was watching a goose being strangled for Christmas dinner. Then she broke out in a smile and asked,

"Have you got a light?"

That put me back on my feet.

"Ah. . . . ."

I sniffed and searched my pocket for a lighter.

". . . Thanks."

She said as she exhaled smoke.

I stood there not being able to decide whether to leave or stay. Stay for what? So I may be able to have this enchanting girl for a company for a while.

The idea was already too depressing. I could delight nobody. . . .

Yet I kept myself there. Something was pulling me to stay. I thought I ought give her some plausible excuse of my flurry, of my crying face.

I cleared my throat quietly.

"—It makes me feel very awkward your standing there like that," the girl said, with some kind of accent.

"It's like I'm a child being scolded by an old maid."

I laughed. Her giggling face beamed in girly mischief. I

started to notice that the glacier in my heart was started to thaw. I could feel the trickles coming down its wall lazily yet undoubtedly. Is this real?

"Sit down."

She said, tapping the floor next to her with her long - nailed fingers. She had smooth, slender wrists that were a little out of balance from the rest of her body. They were as if being glued back together a few times like a plaster bust in a art school. So delicate. That somehow made me feel at ease.

I sat down flying high in flutter, apprehension mixed with anticipation as to where she was going take me. It was a thrilling moment. This pretty girl wants to talk to me!—I began to feel better about myself already. I even felt I had mastered English!

I was about to ask her, for a opener, why she was here in the hallway alone when she said,

"It's a boring party isn't it?" in Japanese.

Taikutsu na paatii janai?—I was completely struck by surprise.

"Why! You speak Japanese!" I screeched in exhilaration.

"What are you saying? Of course I do."

"Japanese?"

"A hundred percent", she said collectedly.

"Wow, but you don't look like one."

The comment seemed to have delighted her immensely—she gave a big toothy smile.

"It might be that my mother is from Nagasaki. Who knows, it could be an atavism."

She surmised proudly.

In the past and present, I'd seen many Japanese girls

who look slightly foreign—every feature of their face is well-defined than regular Japanese girls. But in her case it was truly remarkable. More Polynesian than Japanese. By looking at her up close I noticed that her intense stare was not intentional. She had a pair of particularly wide brown eyes which were set very close to willfully straight eyebrows. Altogether they gave an expression of slight scowl, along with Betty Page hair cut. They reminded me of Anna Karina.

"I'm Satomi, what's your name?"

"Kira."

I wasn't sure if I heard it right.

"Kira, like *Twinkle Twinkle Little Star*?"

"No, don't ask. It's just a nickname."

She let out smoke and grounded the cigarette onto the floor.

A group of people came out of the room laughing, headed for the elevator. One of them, a girl with dark curly maine, saw Kira and stooped over her.

"I've gotta go, but call me. Let's do some lunch."

"O.K. ."

Kira responded with a smile. They exchanged kisses. I watched them admiringly.

"You look like you've been here for a long time."

I said after the girl had left.

"What? On this floor?"

"No, not *here*, I mean in New York."

"Oh, . . . ," she said, looking a little disappointed.

"For three years."

Is that all?—I thought. I'd been here for three years too. Though she appeared to be a lot more confident—more

Americanized than I was for sure. In the way she sat, her gestures, self-assurance was apparent. A little jealous bug stung me.

"I've got a husband, a tom cat, and a second grade abacus diploma."

"Abacus!"

We both laughed.

"Do you want to know how many years I got, too?"

She said with a little mockery.

". . . Well, not unless you want to . . . "

I was more than curious, but I said what I felt I should say.

"I like you."

She said and smiled.

5

I guess any relationship between people involves a balance of power. There is always the one who draws in the other and the one being drawn by the other. There is the one who tells stories and the one who listens. The two never possess equal power.

I wonder if this imbalance has got something to do with aura: if it's our human nature to follow the person who has more forceful aura than ourselves. Just like working bees tag after a queen bee.

Once in a while you meet somebody who has 'funny face'. She is not quite pretty in the common sense but has sacred charm about her that's so untangible you can't put your finger on. It's all in the air she carries. Isn't that what the strong aura—charisma is? And sometimes for some particular people, aura gets to be so powerful it becomes visible to the others—a halo. Jesus had one. Buddha had one. Perhaps Mohammed had one, too. Every god and saint of the world had one. And we gravitate blindly toward them, whether we will it or not. . . .

Or sometimes in other cases, our personal relationships could be based on material possession. One follows the other with more money.

When you are short changed in both material and spritual strength, your life could be pretty limited. You could be a excrement that trails after a goldfish as long as you live.

6

When you come in from lunch time Fifth Avenue traffic, this Japanese bookstore is like an oasis.

The air is dry, temperature never too cool nor too warm, B. G. M. from FM radio wafts between the solitary figure of browsers, barely audible. It's like a manufestation of quintessential Japanese image—rock gardens and tea ceremony; everything is neutral, therefore everything is in peace, that sort of thing—an aesthetic we'd like the rest of the world to adopt. (Not me personally.)

Fifth Avenue, for every once in a while for a few minutes, is fine with me. The number of people there and their pace remind me of Tokyo a little. I know most Downtowners seem to absolutely loathe Midtown, but sometimes (again, I emphasize!—not so often) to have to walk dodge around the people gives me a joy. I get a kick from not being able to walk straight.

I love coming to this book store. Just for the fact they have volume after volume of books and magazines. I could spend all day all night in here, just thumbing through any one of them that I'm interested in. Not that I'm a ferocious reader but imagining having access to all these imformation gives me goose bumps. It must be the similar kind of sentiment Kira feels about clothes. Being surrounded by them one feels spirited, ready to face the world.

Actually, in the past I thought about getting a job here. The pay wasn't so great but I thought if they had some kind of staff discount on books it would balance out. The books here are super expensive, otherwise. However in the end, even before I found out about staff discount I gave the idea a pass. There are so many Japanese restaurants in this city but only two or three Japanese bookstores: If you make an enemy of them and can't come back here for browsing, you'd be terribly sorry. I must say it was a very good judgement of my part.

I took a glimpse at every cover of women's magazines on display. It seemed every time I come here one more new magazine is yet being published. Almost all of them target office girls. Girls with steady job must be a growing market over there.

Though it was lunch time, the store was very quiet today. Usually by this time—quarter to two—the place is crowded with businessmen who are killing a few minutes before heading back to the office. Or worse yet, the place could be bombarded by a big group of Japanese tourists. For some reason, most of the time they tend to be middle aged women (the ratio is like five females to every male), who'd show off the strong example of what collective behavior is. Having no fear, especially when they are in their native element (there must be a psychological explanation to this—'cathartic reaction to being intimidated by skyscrapers and English speakers—something like that), they'd push and shove, and exclaim in hysteria,'my God! these prices are insane!' They'd do the same in restaurants. It's hell sometimes when you work in a Japanese restaurant near big hotels. . . .

Snooping around me briefly, I pluck a teen fashion magazine. A girl who looked like she worked in a travel agency gave me a double take. I pretended not to have noticed her. You need a courage to take a teen mag in hands at the ripe age of twenty-nine. If you look like you're in fashion biz you could get away with it (you're doing a market research, right?), but obviously I don't look the part. Only fashionable thing I have on was my combat boots which none of these office girls would ever dream as chic.

Having had enough of magazines, I moved toward a *bunko* section in the back of the store. I passed the aromatic coffee bar, *shinsho* shelves and children's book section. It was my first time here to see anybody in this otherwise deserted section.

A pretty mother and a child were seemingly deciding over which book to take home. The mother seemed to have her mind set on a book, but the child wasn't sold for the idea.

"But these cats are ugly!" I heard the child say. The way she said was so obnoxious. Well loved and spoiled. Just for a curiousity I took a glimpse to see what kind of a kid she was. Were she not pretty, her behavior would be unforgivable. As I stole a look at her, the mother's eyes met mine. Do I know her?—was the first thing I thought. I felt I was surfacing to a half blank state, as if being woken up from a nod by a tap on the shoulder. Then the white-wash fogginess slowly dispersed.

"Satomi. . . .!?"

"No! Mihoko!?"

No sooner did she call my name than I recognized her. Mihoko Kawashima, my high school class mate.

" Wow! It's too uncanny for an accident!"

"Really!" We looked at each other, surely impressed with fate's oddity.

Two girls from the same high school in suburban Tokyo run each other after eleven years, not in a local drive-in restaurant, but in NEW YORK? Is it true that the universe still keeps expanding and not contracting?

"Ah, it's just so unbelievable! I've heard you've been living in America, but. . . ." Mihoko said, with her cheek glowing from excitement.

"Who told you that?"

I was flattered to hear SOMEBODY in this world brought my name up in their conversation.

"Oh . . . I don't know, who was it . . . ?"

"Never mind. But it's so nice to see you. You live here too, I take it?"

"Yeah, in upstate. For about a year now since my *shujin* was sent to a branch here." Her eyes shined lively.

I was shocked to hear the word 'shujin' come out the mouth of someone of my age. I thought the word (which means the master of the household; therefore one's husband) has long been dead.

". . . Are you married then?"

I didn't even know why I'd asked that.

". . . .Yes?"

She affirmed in bewilderment, then smiled at the child who was hiding behind her mother's skirt, as if to say 'why do you ask?'.

Feeling obliged, I squatted down.

"Hi, there, what's your name?"

The girl moved her head like a mollusk in an educational video on natural life, while giggling shyly. She sure was a cute little thing, taking very much after her mother, down to her apple red cheeks.

"Umm . . . ?"

I peered into her acorn eyes.

"She's so pretty, isn't she?"

I looked up and told the mother. She *was* pretty but I said so feeling somewhat compelled.

"You can answer that yourself, right? Tell Auntie what your name is," the mother demanded softly.

"Auntie . . . "

The voice of both resignation and objection shrieked at the same time.

"Oh, sorry," she chuckled,"Just I associate with so few younger women that calling any female 'auntie' becomes habit. 'Sis' is better, isn't it?"

"If you can spare me."

We laughed. The girl laughed too, but I doubted if she grasped anything. She would have so many years ahead of her after all.

"O.K., so let's tell Sis your name. Your name is—"

The little girl was still swinging her mother's skirt, loving the attention she was getting.

"C'mon, 'my name is——'"

"Mayu," she whispered.

Finally!, I thought, relieved.

"How old is she?" I asked the mother directly this time.

"Going to be three in September. Right, Mayu?"

Mihoko gently stroked the girl's hair, being more than captivated with her creation. There seemed to be not even a slight space between them. Vacuum packed. I guess that's how it is between a mother and a child.

". . . So, what do you do?"

Mihoko asked, raising her head from the child.

"Umm . . ," I drew a deep breath, then let it out quickly, "*Right now*, part-time jobs."

I said it as if sometime in a near future everything would change for the better, like I'd have some artistic career or something. God, I hate to be asked that question. I wish I could call myself 'an artist', just because I paint once in a while. But I felt too guilty and too sorry for myself, just as when I see a self-acclaimed actress who never gets a part.

Mihoko may have sensed something behind my curt reply for she didn't ask any further. Then after a little pause she invited me to her place.

" It's not as far as you think, you know? It'll be wonderful if you could. Maybe next week, what do you say?"

"Wonderful."

To tell the truth, I was a little taken aback by her forwardness. Eleven years between us. My eleven and her eleven.

We exchanged our phone numbers. When she handed

me hers I noticed her last name has changed. The Mihoko Kawashima whom I knew had become Mihoko Matsuda the mother.

After we said good-bye to each other I felt dizzy. I felt like I'd been left out of the steady flow of time. I certainly was with it when I was living in Japan, but now I seemed strayed from it. As of Mihoko must've gone to girls-only junior college, worked a few years as a office girl, then got married and had a child. But I. . . .?

I must have been staring at the sign above the subway window that said 'KARMA CONDITIONED CAR—PLEASE WATCH YOUR BEHAVIOR' for a long time until I finally realized it was a joke. Someone had put an identical looking decal with a different message on the top of the real one, where it was supposed to say AIR-CONDITIONED CAR. It made me laugh, and at that I remembered I'd managed to forget to buy a Japanese community paper: that was what I went to the book store for in the first place.

7

We weren't that close; Mihoko and I. As a matter of fact we hardly knew each other at a personal level in spite of being class mates for two consecutive years. While most of the kids belonged to a group within the class, she pretty much stayed alone. During the lunch break when most of us girls gossiped or took turns in playing a counseller to the others on their kiddy love affair, Mihoko would sit in her seat (third from the front, second from the window) quietly doing something—perhaps reviewing some notes for the afternoon class. Though I'm not quite sure. I remember she was always at her seat looking down at the desk, but what for, I have no idea. She wasn't reading a book for sure, because if she was I would have tried to find out the title out of curiousity. As far as I know she could have been reading a score for her piano lesson. (I didn't know if she actually played piano but she had that image—well brought up middle class maiden, sitting erect in front of the instrument, while her mother made afternoon tea on the doily-covered tabletop.)

Somehow she was very good at not giving away any hints

of what she was like: she never said or did anything surprising or remarkable.

But she was a pretty girl, and that's a factor you could get a lot of milage out of. I knew there were at least three boys who had a desperate crush on her. And many more thought she was more than just acceptable. When our class staged *King Lear* for the school festival, she was voted in to play the role of Cornelia by a wide margin.

Her lily-of-the-valley like neat and cleaness—for she always had her shoulder length hair pulled back with a black head band, and her well developed body in convent school type jumper skirt—along with her tendancy to blush easily gave her a mysterious air of transcendence, like she was sacred. The shy boys went for it, and girls agreed on she was pretty and nice.

So it was a surprise when she invited me to her place following a brief encounter after so many years. If we had run each other in Tokyo, we would have only exchanged greetings, chatted for a while (she would compliment on my robustness or whatever, and I in return would do the same by saying nice thing about her little girl), and parted without exchanging our phone numbers. But here in America, living the life of transplanted, we all seem to be in need of one another, others who can share the minor frustrations and homesickness with, in the language we know every nuance of.

This country's land out there must be immense, but from

our eyes we can see clearly where it ends. We are like sheep enclosed in an invisible fence. Only the brave can go out there and make a mark.We all dream of becoming the one eventually, but in the meantime flock together just to survive within the fence.

8

I look up at the clock behind a porcelain Welcome Cat. 9:05. Two more hours till closing time. I sigh. It's only Tuesday and the place is packed.

"Grilled salmon to No.12, shrimp gyoza to No.5!"

Erika calls, while matching the order notes to dishes. She's fully in charge of this place.

"And, Satomi-san, don't forget extra plate for No.4"

Now and then it gets to you to be ordered around by someone obviously a lot younger than yourself. Erika must be twenty-one or thereabout, looks straight out of high school.

I'd need a couple more days to get my waitressing knack back. I hate to admit but sometimes it's easier being told what to do. Though that's something I really don't want to get use to.

As I put the gyoza down on the table, I notice they were from frozen packets available from the Korean deli around the corner, not homemade, as they are described in the menu. The back of my ear itch. I am not one-hundred-percent sure, but I know the shape too well. I set the plate in front of the stylish-looking customer. She looks at it, gives an affirming nod, and splits the chopsticks.

—She doesn't know—I let out a sigh of relief.

As long as the customer is happy, we should be happy, too.

"Excuse me!"

I turn around to see who is calling.

"Excuse me."

A Japanese guy, rich college kid type, raises his hand.

"One moment, please," I tell him, and hurry to the kitchen to return a couple of dirty sushi platforms.

"Yes? What can I do for you?"

I walk up to the guy's table.

"Is hers ready yet?"

The guy asks, pointing with his chin to the empty space in front of his dinner companion. She is a pretty brunette.

"What did you order?" I try to be decent.

"Sushi-sashimi combo," she says regretfully.

I glance at the bar counter which has been filled up completely for last hour or so.

"Let me see."

I go up to the sushi bar where Mr. Ikeda, the owner, is turning up nicely proportioned sushi by swift movement of his hands.

"Is the sushi-sashimi combo for No.8 ready yet?"

I ask him while arrest my eyes on the fleshy salmon on the cutting board. I gulp down saliva. I remember I haven't had anything since lunch.

"Umm . . . , wait a sec," he runs his eyes through the orders without ceasing the movement.

"It's gonna be fifteen, no, ten minutes. Ten minutes."

"O.K.."

I go back to table No.8, a little anxious.

"Sorry for keeping you waiting, but it's going to be another ten minutes."

"Ten munites!"

The guy hits the roof.

"You gotta be kidding, ten munites! What am I supposed to do during that time? Why can't you take care to serve both of us at the same time? It's ridiculous. You could have told me beforehand that sushi would take that long—"

"I'm very sorry," I say, for not knowing whatelse to say, but feeling unfairly accused. I didn't take his order in the first place.

"If you wish us to take your plate away for now—"

"Oh, Takashi—"

As I start dreading, the brunette, who's been left out of our exchange in Japanese, interjects.

"It's O.K. . Look, this place is packed, obviously they're really busy. I'm afraid we came at the peak time. I can wait. Just start yours, please. It's no big deal."

The brunette girl caps off and smiles at me to assure that she's not ruffled.

"Thank you."

I say, and bow.

" Satomi-san, do you know what Samurai Sunrise is?"

When a lull comes to the restaurant, Erika asks me.

"You mean the drink?"

"You knew!" she exclaims.

"Why, did somebody ask you for it?" I ask with an air of authority.

“Yes. You know the guys who were at No.14, the corner table—”

Actually I did notice them—three guys, all in mid fifties, still in their business suit—probably on their business trip to the city. Rare customers in this neighborhood.

“They asked me.”

She keeps on.

“At first I had no idea what he was talking about, so I said, ‘excuse me? what can I get you?’ Then the guy drew out ‘Samurai Sunrise’ again, to make sure I understood. So by this time I figured that it must be the name of a drink or something so I said, ‘sorry, sir, but we don’t have it. We have sake, beer, plum wine . . .’ Then he went, ‘No Samurai Sunrise? Isn’t this a Japanese restaurant?’ ”

“You don’t hear about it much, but I think it was once a popular drink.”

I say, though I am not sure. I only know it exists.

“Those people are from the crack of the butt, aren’t they?”

Yuya, who was listening from behind the cashier island, butts in.

“What’s the crack of the butt?” I ask. Never heard that expression.

“You see, when you look at a two-page spread map of this country, the places that are so close to the binding that you can’t see without pulling the pages wide open—Oklahoma, Kansas, Nevada—”

“Nevada is next to California.” Erika says.

“Is it? Right, viva Las Vegas! That’s right, I mean is—”

“Nebraska?” I say.

“That’s it. Nebraska. . . .You know in those places they

make no distinction of various Asians. They're aware that there are Japanese, Chinese, Korean, but somehow they think we are all the same."

"But I can't tell a Dutch from a Portuguese," I say.

"But you know the difference between tempura and—what's Holland famous for except tulips?—I can't think of any dish. . . .Anyway, an American's idea of Japanese food includes wonton soup and Peking Duck. And the other way around: when they are at a Chinese restaurant they expect Sushi on the menu . . . "

"They do? I've never heard such a thing."

Erika frowns credulously. She looks like a teenager protesting at her smart alec brother.

"It's true! Only in New York things are different. People have a better idea of different ethnicities. But outthere, in the middle, no way. Japanese restaurants do serve Peking Duck—because they are more likely be owned by Chinese. That really makes things worse, in terms of distinguishing one nation's dish from the next. I bet those guys learned about Samurai Sunrise at Trader Vics or somewhere like that."

"Trader Vics!"

Erika and I burst out laughing.

". . . So you've been 'outthere'?"

Erika asks Yuya.

"No, not myself, but I have a friend in Minnesota."

"Minnesota, hmmm. I prefer my own private Idaho . . . Keanu!" Erika screams jovialy. She seems to be picking up energy for an after-work outing.

"But, wait," I plunge in,

"We do eat ramen or curry a lot, don't we? Although

they aren't indigenous, since we eat them perhaps more often than we eat sushi they got to be called typical Japanese dishes. Not sushi or sashimi. But in reality, Japanese restaurants rarely serve them, like these dishes are too low-brow or something. Isn't it right? Don't you think we misrepresent ourselves by selling some expensive dish like sashimi as our very typical food? So we can say our taste in every way is a lot superior to others'? So we can laugh at Americans for eating so many hamburgers and pizza all the time?"

I feel good about finishing off my speech. Erica and Yuya gape at me.

"Hey, you guys, No.6 wants a check."

Mr. Ikeda's stern voice breaks us up.

"Certainly."

I put the check on the black plastic tray with American Express logo.

Don't leave home without it—Whatever happened to the ad? I wonder.

"Thank you very much," I put down a check on the table with a smile, minding not to overdo it.

"Thank you very much, *arigatogozaimashita*!"

Mr. Ikeda calls out to the door where the Japanese guy and the brunette are leaving.

"Thank you," I say halfheartedly, and go to their table to collect the check.

The guy left fifty dollars even for the check of $49.50.

9

All the way to the stop I was supposed to get off I'd been nervous. Mihoko had told me over the phone that there's only one train per every hour in either direction; in other words once you missed to get off you'd be screwed. So I got uneasy every time the train reached a station.

"About an hour out of Grand Central," she had told me, and my nervousness reached its peak about fifty minutes into the journey. I started to worry whether I had missed the stop.

But just as she said, in a few munites the train glided into a platform which bore the name of the station I recognized.

As I came out of the station, I noticed the bareness of the area. I mean there were woods but somehow I'd expected to see a typical suburban street that stretched from the rotary which offered basic services such as dry cleaners and groceries. Local kids could be hanging around in front of an ice cream parlor, licking their favorite flavor, still straddled on a bicycle. But that scenery was typical only in my head. All around me was a thicket of assorted trees which appeared as real as a mammoth's tusk I'd seen long ago in a museum. They had an assertiveness of predecessers. A lonely stretch of narrow road wound uphill through them. I felt like I had traveled long way from home.

"Satomi."

A white Honda Accord pulled up next to me.

"Sorry, did you wait for long?"

Mihoko stuck out her head from the driver's seat. Half of her face was obscured with huge glasses. For driving only, I figured.

"No, just got here."

"Good. I couldn't have lost you here. I had to mess with the safety seat. . . ."

She nodded at the girl in the back. She seemed to be in a good mood.

"Hi, Mayu-chan."

I waved and she shyly giggled back at me.

"C'mon, get in," Mihoko beckoned.

Her house was on a neat tree lined street. Very American as I've seen in the movies. All the houses had their own styles (sort of), though there was a peculiar uniformity to the street. Maybe it's that every house started at certain distance from the property line as if they were racing horses readying in their gates, each marked by a mail box.

Inside was, the best I could describe as sparse. Sparsity of wastefulness. Everything in here had its serving purpose—no useless personal objects that people tend to accumulate for one reason or the other. It was almost stoic like a hotel room for its determination not to appear personable, only in this house nobody seemed to have paid any attention to the proportions: A long couch sat in a equally eel-like living room, an enormous glass-top dining table occupied the entire kitchen area.

"They are all rentals," Mihoko said, somehow apologetically.

"I see. . . .Hmm. . . ."

I wanted to say something more but I lost it.

While Mihoko prepared for lunch I went through photo albums she had brought out of the bedroom. They consisted of three volumes of serious thickness. They started from the wedding, then of course, honeymoon (in Hawaii), various indoor shots, small outings and trips, and so went on. A lot of them were shots of Mihoko alone until the baby's birth; after that both mother and father seemed eager to take turns to be photographed with the baby, or forced a camera to a third person so that they could be photographed together with the baby.

Mihoko's husband had a nice reliable smile of an elite banker. A self-assured smile. Although she'd told me he was only two years older than us, from these pictures he looked well five years ahead of us. Something about him reminded me of my last boyfriend Mark. My heart was wrung a bit. Although it'd been more than a year since we broke up, I still thought about him from time to time, which was unthinkable at the time of our break up. . . .But you can't do anything about it now.

As I was almost tumbling into a dense fogginess, Mihoko called me from the kitchen.

"Thank you for waiting."

* * *

The lunch was absolutely wonderful. I'd have given her a ten if I was a contest judge. It had a grilled fish, a couple of vegetable dishes, sunomono, miso soup, rice and pickles—(she apologized for not making anything special, just like a typical family supper!). This much variety is something you can only manage when you have somebody to sit with you and appreciate your effort everyday. What a lucky guy her husband is! And Mihoko too, for having a nice husband who complements her. I had a feeling that Mihoko could be a pretty good cook even way back when. (That's probably what everybody in our class thought: Mihoko would be an ideal wife.) When I told her that she blushed a bit and after a little while told me she had gone to a crash course on cooking.

"Crash course?"

"Uh-huh. It's a nine-to-five cooking lesson where you learn basics. To grill, to fry, to stew. . . .It's mainly designed for people who are in a hurry to make the deadline."

"Deadline?"

"The wedding."

"Oh."

I was a trifle staggered by her matter-of-factness. She wasn't like this in school; or at least *I* wasn't close enough to know her being this way. For me she always remained as a pretty but docile, attractive to the eyes but maybe too mechanical.

Mihoko busily arranged coffee cups and saucers. She put cup handle to the left, handle of spoon to the right, a la Japanese manner school, and let out in one breath,

"We married by match making."

She kept her eyes on her knuckles.

"Oh, really."

I said as if a match-making marriage was the most common thing in the world as flu or umbrellas on a rainy day. Though I didn't show, I was quite surprised, of course. You'd imagine somebody as pretty as Mihoko, who also appeared gentle and obedient, must have been very popular. She wasn't a lover-mistress type; she was the one you'd want to wait for you at home, if you were a man. Yet the one such as she had to go through this process to get married? I began to wonder if I might have misconceived her completely from the beginning: she may had a persona that I was incapable of picturing from her navy uniform.

"Do you remember Sugano?"

Minoko asked, setting down a coffee cup before me.

"Who's that?"

"You don't remember? Sugano from football circle?"

"Oh, yes! yes!"

Sugano, the handsome quaterback who was two years senior of us. Everybody knew him. He was one of those guys who was popular among the boys for his straight forward character and among the girls for his sweet nature. . . . God, it's been a long time—I started flow into the sea of nostalgia.

"I was going with him for four years."

Mihoko peered into my face as if to see my reaction.

"Really? I had no clue."

I pictured the two together walking down the street. A perfect looking couple. Almost exceedingly so.

" No, not during the high school. After. We had a mutual acquaintance—Kishida, from our class. You remember him, don't you?"

"Of course!"

Her mentioning his name brought me back the guy who cracked hopeless jokes one after another in front of the whole class. He was a class 'A' class clown. He also used to sell me the movie tickets his family got for free in exchange for offering their property fence for putting up movie posters.

"Kishida and Sugano—I wonder what they are doing now. I wonder if Sugano is still really handsome. . . ."

I smiled at Mihoko to see if she wanted to comment on that, but she only made a little troubled face.

"Kishida is a phys-ed teacher in a high school, as far as I know. . . .but Sugano, I wonder what he's doing now myself. . . ."

Mihoko started to give me an account of her relationship with Sugano; how they had met in a picnic, how they had wonderful days together until it all came to a halt by Sugano's loss of his self motivation—as she put it.

"It was fun when he was still in college. Every weekend I'd go see him play, afterwards we'd either join the team fo a party or walk around a little till we ended up in a coffee house. He was always so animated from the game. Full of energy. That was a wonderful time. Until. . . ."

I started wonder why she wanted to tell me all this, about her seemingly bitter past with this guy. Why me? I haven't seen her in so long, and had never been her close friend or anything. I waited if she was going to change the topic but she stayed on, as if talking to herself out loud.

"I don't know why, whenever I look back then, the time I had with Sugano, I end up feeling terrible. I can't keep my memory with just the nice things, nice time we had. I always remember him as sad. . . . . ."

I somehow had the feeling this was something she kept to herself for a long time, the door shut tight and triple locked. And now, perhaps once and for all she wanted to let it all go. To relieve herself—from guilt. I was a perfect opportunity, perhaps, I knew her but not well enough. I let her continue.

"There had always been a sign after he graduated college—as I look back. Small complaints about his work, his lack of interest in going out on weekends. Like dust accumulates without my knowledge, we eventually got to the point where neither of us was able to breathe when the other was around."

Mihoko held her cup with her both hands, and stared at the liquid inside. She may have been staring at the reflection of her pained face.

"We tried to repair it, but somewhere in our mind we both were feeling there's no remedy. He'd blame himself first for his ineptness, then me for not caring enough about him. . . .Every time we argued we'd come back to the same spot, only we got more and more weary. . . .'till I finally decided to leave him. He'd become someone else. I knew he was torn between his ideal and reality. He'd say 'I may lie to you but I don't want to lie to myself,' stuff like that. I mean I understood. But as we get to a certain age we are expected to act a certain way, isn't that right? You may have to trick yourself into lying. . . .You know, sometimes I think if he hadn't been a star in school, if he was a plain Joe, he wouldn't have had to go through all these disappointments in a 'real life', probably. He could've taken everything as it came. But he was too hung up on being a . . . I don't know . . . it's not his fault if he was the way he was. But then, what is and what isn't one's fault?"

She looked at me in the eye, a little feverish, wanting to be forgiven. I searched for words but nothing came out of my mouth. She kept her eyes on me for a while, then shook her head.

"I'm sorry. I didn't mean to put you on the spot."

She tried a smile but it didn't come off convincingly.

"You know the funny thing is he used to talk a lot about 'going to America', leaving everythinig behind, me included. But now look *who* is here. It's a little ironical, isn't it? Sometimes I feel you can't navigate the life at your own will, isn't that true?"

I still didn't know anything to say that was worthwhile.

"Anyway, why don't I make some more coffee?"

She said cheerfully and got up.

While waiting for the water to boil, she switched to talk about how limited the closest supermarket was. It was like a curtain was being drawn, to say the performance was over. Now she could go back to her ordinary life, shutting off everybody from internal ongoings.

She was again the same Mihoko Kawashima from Akebono High.

The phone rang. Mihoko became alert and picked up the reciever.

" Hello—*moshi moshi*, Matsuda's residence."

She answered in a dressed-up receptionist-like voice.

I looked out the window at the neglected lawn in front of the house, where sun-beaten toy car was ditched near the fence with its belly up. The water from last rain sat on the hollow of plastic floorboard. Everything was dead still. No cars, no children, not even a dog walker. Only the leaves near the top of the trees brushed against one another, scattering the light through.

Mihoko hung up the phone with a little bow. I was impressed with her fluency in honorific. Half-mockingly she let out a sigh.

"You seem to have quite a lot of obligations," I teased her.

"You said it. That call was about the arrangement for next Thursday—a weekly tea party of businessmen's wives which I am going to host. Before that, on Wednesday I have English lessons, Mayu's school on Mondays.

"What do you mean by 'school' ?" I was totally astonished.

" It's kind of pre-kindergarden play-class, where they teach kids a little arithmetic and to read and write alphabets, Japanese and English, and so on."

She said with satisfactory smile.

"But don't you think it's too early?" I ventured. I couldn't picture arithmetic could be a 'play'.

"Oh, no," her face become animated,

"Everybody, I mean, every kid does this these days. It's not exactly my choice . . . Do you know a three-year-old kid has three-hundred-percent more learning ability than a six-year-old? There's no such time as too early."

I could only nod.

"Besides all the kids in Japan do much more than the kids here. I want to make sure the transition goes smoothly for Mayu when we go back to Japan. I don't want her to feel she's behind. Right now, because of this class and home work, she has a capacity of nearly four and half - year-old, the test showed, so I want to keep it up."

She obviously took a pride in her little daughter.

"Umm. What you say makes sense, I guess," though I wasn't so sure,

"But doing well in school isn't everything."

What the point of blindly following 'just do what every-body does' policy and bring her up as 'one of many'—you can look at me and figure it out.

"Kids can learn a lot from picking flowers, playing with other kids . . . "

"I know you want to say 'kids should play more', but at this time and age. . . .Perhaps you'll understand when you have children yourself."

She made a sorrowful face, with an exaggeration, as if to say 'why can you understand, I'm doing this only for love of my daughter, not for anything else. Frankly I didn't care so much about what she put her kid through, but the way she attempted to make herself look like an un-self-centered-person ever so subtly started to rub me the wrong way. This sense of self-cuddling goodness—now I found a name for after all these years—probably was the reason I kept the distance from her in the school days.

"Yeah, I suppose I won't know anything until I get there." I said.

"Mama. . . .,"

A half-asleep face of the child appeared from the kitchen.

"Oh, you're up,"Mihoko said and looked up at the clock on the wall. Five twenty-five. It was about time for me to go home.

"Come here."

Mihoko called the child, and the she responded by playfully falling on her lap.

"Wait, wait!" she cheerfully made a fuss. The child's face was all wet.

"Do *cheen*, Mayu," Mihoko covered the child's face with a tissue.

"Cheeeen!" the child blew her nose.

"Good girl."

Mihoko smiled at her as if nothing else existed in the whole world.

The child started hum some song—something about a rabbit—while being finger-combed the hair by her mother. The child was most charming in her delirious state.

"Mama, Papa home yet?"

"Not yet," Mihoko answered in a singing tone.

I watched their exchange with a slight envy for a while then decided to leave. There should be a train at ten after six.

"I think I gotta go."

"No, really? Could you stay for dinner? My husband'll be back soon, he'll be delighted to meet you."

"Umm . . . It's really nice of you but . . . "

I pictured surrounding the table with her husband. The idea of having to have to talk to an elite banker made my shoulder tense. He could be a nice guy, on the other hand, he could treat me nicely as a drop-out, a failure—it could be my paranoia but I longed for my own place.

"—I really mean it, if you're worried about the train home, he'd be able to drive you home."

She looked at me wholeheartedly.

"I'm sorry, but I have to go. I'm expecting a phone call from my mother."

I lied, and that left me a bitter taste in my mouth. From out of nowhere, I suddenly felt huge compassion for her, not from the lie, but for her—what? For her to await her husband's return everyday. Maybe.

"Come visit me again, will you?"

She said as she she dropped me off at the station. She was being very sincere.

"Oh, for sure. You, too, call me when you come into the city, O.K.?"

"Sure. Thank you."

Her politeness.

". . . .Well, then, see you."

"Yes, stay in touch, see you."

"Bye-bye, Mayu-chan."

I waved though I couldn't see her from the reflection of the window.

After their car had gone, I was left there not just with the sense of relief I'd expected but also a reluctance to leave the place and go back to the city alone, where nobody waited.

10

Kira called and invited me to a play.

"A play?"

I asked because I thought Kira didn't like plays. She loved movies(that was something I shared her interest with), but not plays. She once told me that she had a difficulty getting into them for, unlike movies, she couldn't get rid of the idea that what she was seeing were actors, not characters.

"Movies are ultimately perfect make-beliefs, a fiction that can carry you through the different lives and different world by wardrobes and actual, not a cardboard, sceneries—you *know* you're not there with those characters, you're only sitting in this tiny, angled seat. But they have a way to let you forget about that. . . .But plays, (she stuck her tongue out) sometimes you can smell their musty costumes," she had said before.

"A play?"

When I scrutinized her for what she said, she put her foot down.

"Don't be so skeptical. You heard it right. We are going to see a play Stephen's friend directed."

"Oh."

"Be here by seven, O.K.?"

Then she hung up.

When I got to her place, Stephen opened the door. Though I expected see him here I was kind of taken aback nonetheless. I'd become used to this place as Kira's.

"Satomi,"he smiled.

"Stephen," I smiled.

We stood there in a mutual affection, perhaps both deciding whether to kiss each other or not.

"Come in."

We decided not to. I was kind of relieved by it, but at the same time felt a little bit like being classified as a heathen.

Stephen led me into the apartment I already knew quite well: a glassed roof, leopard couch along the scenic windows, Venetian lamps, and Kira's collection of bird cages in the den.

"Kira, Satomi's here."

Stephen called out, and I heard Kira acknowledge him from the bedroom.

"Same as always."

Stephen said with insipid endurance, referring Kira's eternal dressing-up procedure. I smirked as a sign of agreement.

"Wow, how pretty."

Outside of the window, a pink sliver of the sky was sinking slowly under the frothy weight of early summer night. Miles Davis's 'The Sketch of Spain' cascaded through the living room, making this place feel like a hanging garden. The cat yawned and stretched in a armchair.

"Sit down, why don't you, and I'll make you a drink—what would you like?"

"Umm . . . "

As usual I haven't got a preference. Almost anything would do.

"Beer, wine, juice,. . . .I'm having a gin tonic. Would you like that?"

He knew of my indecisiveness.

"Sounds good."

"Good."

He made an ambiguous smile and disappeared into the kitchen area.

I slid myself deeper into the couch, and let my eyes roam around the room. Yet nothing seemed to have rearranged in obvious way, the room has changed since last time I was here. It appeared distant, almost putting on airs. It was an odd feeling, like you found yourself sitting in a minutely executed forgery after you spent time with the original. A few minutes later it dawned on me that Kira's usual existential trace had been missing—no shirt slouched off a dining chair, no pieces of cotton balls lying on a floor. King Stephen must have taken his domain back from the lazy queen.

Stephen came back with gin tonics (swizzle stick, lime and all)and handed one to me.

"Thank you."

"Pleasure."

He made a gentleman-like small bow, then sat down on the couch opposit from me. As he bent his knees, big faces of crowned frogs appeared between his pantlegs and loafers. For a brief moment I wondered if it signified anything. I was pretty positive they had been picked up by Kira, for they looked a little too dorky for Stephen, or for any man for that matter. I'm not sure if I'd want to go date with a guy who would wear those socks. Not that I was in a position to be choosy, but it's an important factor.

I kept stirring the drink with a tiny plastic sword for lack of things to do. I watched Stephen take a sip from the glass.

Still no sign of Kira emerging out of the bedroom. I was getting a little uncomfortable.

"So."

"So?"

After a visible sigh, he turned to me. We seemed to have a tacit understanding of each other's discomfort.

"So . . . How was the trip?"

For once I decided to toss an opener. Into my head came an image of me throwing a fishline in a half-dried pond. I really never know what to say to Stephen.

"Good. Real good, actually."

He nodded in satisfaction, with a smile that made him look boyish, kind of cute.

"You were gone for a while, weren't you?"

"Two weeks."

"Is that all? I thought you were gone for at least for a month and a half."

"Well, yeah, it's kind of true. I was here for just a few days in between. . . . ."

He didn't elaborate much, and little by little my mind started side-tracking into a thick haze called deja vu.

I mean, how many times have I gone through this exact conversation with him?

I: How did you like the trip?

S(Stephen): Good.(Pretty good, O.K., etc)

I: You were gone for ages.

S:———(Fill in the length)

It's amazing, the way we both tolerate. We'd see each other, have chitchat over dinner, say good night in friendly affection(with the help of alcohol), and then when we see each other again a few months later, we'd start (awkwardly) all over again. Perhaps a year from now, three years from now we'd be doing the same thing over and over . . . And over and over. . . .until we discover some scientific theory about this. . . .

". . . . . ?"

When I came back to my senses, I saw Stephen looking at me. He must have asked me some question: I was vaguely aware of that. I tried to gather up with all my might what we were talking about, but couldn't remember. I was shocked and embarassed, and totally dismayed. I could feel my heart was pumping out the blood faster than normal, with the speediness and precision of a rice cake maker's assistant. This was the moment that a few second of silence seemed eternal.

I muttered "umm" in order to give him the impression that I was giving his question some serious thought.(My fishline got caught in the crack of the bottom of the pond. . . .)We were talking something about travelling. . . .

beat—beat—beat.

"I'm sorry, I didn't get your question. Could you say that again?"

Finally I ventured out, pretending, so that Stephen might take it as I didn't understand English. A cold sweat broke out in my underarm.

". . . . . . I said, 'have-you-been-to-Ballenas'—"

Stephen drew out the each word deliberately. He was obviously annoyed.

"Oh . . . , ah. . . .,no."

I shook my head, feeling desperate.

Stephen let out a sigh. Again. He seemed to be sighing a lot today.

I wondered if it was *my* doing. Am *I* sending him into this desperate state? Does he think he has to keep me a company?. . . .The sense of guilt was overwhelming. Kira, come out of the bedroom!

". . . . I'm sorry."

I uttered.

"What? What are you sorry for?"

He looked at me, perplexed, as if I had quoted from the teachings of Confucius. He really didn't seem to get it.

". . . .'Cause. . . . ."

I tried to construct a sentence from various fragments that floated around my head simultaneously like balloons in comicbooks.

". . . I thought I may be boring you."

Funny, after I let it out I felt much lighter all of a sudden.

"What? But why? What makes you think that way?"

He peered into my face and shook his head without exactly denying what I'd said.

"Well . . . ," I hesitated for a second, then,

"I've noticed you've been sighing a lot."

"Have I?"

He looked me in the face powerlessly, as if I'd reminded him of an abhorrent childhood secret he had sealed and forgotten. Suddenly He looked exhasted.

". . . . . . ."

He heaved a sigh, and right away realized it.

"Dear me!"

We laughed so hard that Stephen looked almost like he was suffering, and I struggled to put down the glass on the table to keep it from spilling. The gin tonic was rushing through my system in full force. I tried to stretch this laugh as long as posssible.

We must have been laughing for a few minutes until the tidal wave died down and Stephen grew pensive. He let his short curly hair fall over his baby face—the expression of gloom was something I'd never imagined him capable—moody: yes; but gloomy: no. He leaned forward, held his eyes at a point half way between him and floor, lost in thoughts. We sat there like a subject in a Edward Hopper's painting in the background of melancholy resonance of Miles Davis.

Not knowing what to do, I finished up my drink—I had no idea I'd drunk this much already. As I gulped down, the last piece of ice went down my throat like a chipped rock from a cliff top, made me shiver.

"Satomi. . . .,"

Stephen murmured, while he still kept his eyes on the glass between his palms.

"Uh . . . I must be tired than I thought."

He tried to smile just with the corner of the mouth. I felt he had wanted to say something else and decided not to.

"Do you still want to go to the play?"

I knew it wasn't my place to ask, but he did look a bit frazzled.

"Yeah, we're going. . . . Speaking of which, what time is it?"

He looked at his watch.

"Hey, we'd better hurry now. I'll tell Kira."

After a minute or two Stephen walked into the bedroom, I heard them arguing. The door was shut so I couldn't tell what they were saying exactly, but the tone of their exchange was definitely that of a bicker. It probably got to do with Kira's taking so much time to dress up, but I didn't wanna know. . . .

What's happening to everybody today?

Just as I was about to get up and move to the other part of the room to avoid catching anything they were saying, Kira, who was fully made up, stuck her head out of the room.

"Come, Satomi,"

She beckoned. She looked the usual: there was no trace of commotion in her face.

I wasn't exactly thrilled to join the two, but I got up anyway.

"What do you think, huh?"

She spinned around once to show her dress. Stephen went out of the room as I entered.

"Wow, it's beautiful."

It was a A-lined white dress in peculiar kind of nylon. The color was almost iridescent.

"Sooo nice! let me see . ."

I touched the dress around hem; it was incredibly light.

"Helmut Lang," Kira said proudly,

"On sale, of course."

She didn't forget to add "of course."

"—Hey what smell is this?"

I noticed a transfixing scent emanating from Kira. It was floral but rather discreet unlike any I know and despise. It reminded me of a chaste widow.

Kira grinned.

"If you could smell a movie, what Catherine Deneuve was wearing in *Tristana* got to be this one."

She said with magnetic eyes.

11

The play was relatively painless. Unlike Kira, I enjoy plays as much as movies—provided actors speak loud in standard American English, the same way TV newscasters and language instructors in cassettes talk. I have a foreign accent, and I understand other foreign accents pretty well, but American regional accent or English accent, I have a hard time.

One time when I was a student in a E.S.L. school, I went to see a Shakespeare—one of the field trips included in school's grossly high tuition. It was Richard the Third by Royal Shakespeare Company, I believe, but God, was I miserable. The duration of three hours, I was so discouraged by the shortcomings of my comprehension: I didn't understand one word of it. To make the matters worse, I happened to be seated right next to some expert(?), who seemed know every word of the play and enjoying it through and through. . . .I really felt like I was a klutz.

The story of tonight's play went like this: A girl who was going out with a few guys finds out she is pregnant. She tries to determine whose baby she's carrying but doesn't get anywhere. She thinks about getting abortion, but in the end decides not to because she finds it's a personal matter and does not involve the third party—the guy, the father. When she realizes this she becomes liberated, therfore becomes an independet person. . . . .

I was quite intrigued until it came to a sort of glorious ending.

I don't like glorious endings. Actually, for that matter, I don't like anything that ends too solidly. Granted any fiction is a fiction to start with, still, I think the clear-cut ending is phony. After all nothing ends in this world until your heart stops beating. So even to put some tentative period (.) in someone's life feel fake to me. It's a comma (,) not period (.), that should be put down.

I particularly hate love stories that end in dramatic escape. A boy and girl fall in love in spite of the obstacles between them (a class conflict, either's health problems, etc), go through turmoil that nearly separates them, but then, they realize that they can't live a day without each other, jump on a ship for a better future together, leaving everything behind. (Here we hear exalting symphonic music, by some unknown 'small town somewhere' orchestra if it's a movie.) I just can't help wondering about how they're going to live—no money, no checks, where are they going to stay without an I.D.? At least Romeo and Juliet didn't go through such a trite way—that's something to be said about Shakespeare, I guess. But Kira thinks I'm too stodgy and tend to knead some truly trivial things till my hand sticks in a dough. She says to leave entertainment as entertainment.

"Why should we compare fiction to real life? I don't read books or go to movies to sharpen my perception. Give that to dogs, they won't eat it!"

I know she's right.

* * *

A decorative arts dealer and a stage director—I couldn't connect them together at first, though I knew Stephen has wide range of friends. Then Kira told me that they were friends from the art school where Stephen dropped out.

"Hmm. . . ."

Before I heard that I'd pictured him like a caricature image of director—silver hair, beard with a pipe sticking out, camel-colored scarf around the neck (even in the summer). In real life Alex turned out to be a charming, soft-spoken, tall—in other words, quite attractive. He had a peculiar look that refused to give away a clue about his ancestry—too dark for a European, and too angular for an Asian.

"Guatemalan-Russian."

He said with winsome smile when we stood around in a bar where the opening night party was in full swing.

"Russian father, Guatemalan mother."

That really fascinated me. Here was somebody who had two completely unrelated cultural-racial backgound within one body. He could be a Guatemalan with a Russian blood, or Russian with Guatemalan blood, depending on what kind of mood he's in or whichever suitable for the situation

Then above all he was an American. Compare to me who is in every way—Japanese. I envied him.

"So Alex, whatelse have you been working on?"

Kira asked, looking radiant as ever in her white dress. You could see her undeniable cleavage through the deep U-shaped neckline. (Do you still call it a neckline, not a tits line?)

Alex cast his eyes on her with tenderness that was a little more than neutral affection one showed towards a friend's wife.

"Right now I'm working on a film script with Stan Klossowski about Mexican gypsies."

"Mexican gypsies? Are there gypsies in Mexico?"

Stephen asked.

"Yeah, not many left, but there are. They carry a tent and an old projector in the back of a beat up VW van, and set up a makeshift movie theater in a neck of woods—or neck of cacti, I should say. Usually a family, kids'll sell tickets and wife'll be in charge of a concession, tamales and coke, stuff like that, while her husband goes around the village with a totally distorted loudspeaker calling people in until there's enough people to start a show. . . ."

My eyes stuck fast to his feverish eyes. I pictured him following this gypsy family with the same fanaticism. His cheek burnt red from the sun, wiping off sweat with his smooth arm. . . .

"It used to be big excitement for villagers, maybe not as big as Christmas or their patron saint's day, but big enough for them to work extra hours so they could go see the movie. Can you imagine these people have been cut off from any source of information, no daily newspaper, only radio. Then naturally the evil—"

"TV came in and changed their life."

"Exactly."

He acknowledged Stephen.

His story brought my mind *Bye Bye Brazil*, a movie about road-side circus loses its place to television. Alex must be aware of this movie.

"But, doesn't it sound a bit like *Bye Bye Brazil*?"

Kira butted in, acting re*ee*al casual. How dare she, I thought.

But Alex calmly fixed his gaze at her like a priest forgiving a sinner and said,

"It's more like *La Strada* than *Bye Bye Brazil* if you must compare it to something."

"It's not the story that's so impressive, but the way it's told that's intriguing—is that what you're saying?"

"Sometimes."

Then they smiled at each other! Why? What does Alex see in Kira?

"That's my favorite movie of all time—*La Strada*. I must have seen it at least twenty-six times!"

It was a case of 'gone to catch a tiger and came back with a neighbor's hen'. The instant I completed the sentence I regreted it. They all looked at me dumbstruck—Alex, Kira, and even Stephen (can he tame his wife?)—like I was a clueless cousin or a kid who want to poke her head into grownup's conversation.

I only wanted to Alex to know I was there too.

I looked at the pattern of my jeans for God knows how long, 'til forever polite Alex said,

"It was my favorite too. 'Zampano has arrived!'"

He imitated Anthony Quinn drumming his chest with fists. It was enough to send me home happy.

* * *

That night I had a dream. Of me and a guy in bed (actually it was a futon). We were in some rundown Japanese inn—worn out tatami mats, damp futon so thin like a *senbei* cracker. Dim light shone on my naked knees that were pinned in the air, made them look like a pair of hazy spring moon. . . .And I was seething; lubricated, saturated, gasping for the air with every thrust I got, faster, no, more, I get higher and higher, the pinnacle sharper and sharper, I'm burning to get there, take me there, will you? will you? I mutter a few lewd words to make you happy, between, between my moan, that's you can't stop, muffle me, but I won't stop, moan, the words, all that nonsense, I string them like a strand of beads, No! Yes! Yes! take me, let me, please,. . . . . Alex!

I woke up with shame, joy, and disappointment all in one. It was like I'd finally become equal to a hideous middle aged man who would do anything to get his dick sucked for free. No selectiveness, whoever available.

I didn't see why it had to be Alex. He was wonderful and nice and all that, but I wasn't attracted to him sexually. Or is a dream really a realization of your hidden desire? One thing I can save my face is that I didn't see him—I only called his name, thank God. Otherwise everything would be too crude. I can't face it, much less face *him*!

Still, now I wish I'd peaked in the dream. I missed out a good one.

12

When I came home from work, there was a message on my answering machine:

"Hello, Sis, it's Rie. I'm calling to let you know my arrival. I'll be landing in JFK at. . . . . ."

She really is coming to New York.

13

Flankry speaking, I think Kira and Stephen are pretty odd couple. It's not just the way they look—they are both small people and toy-like—but they are like a children's play game sometimes. For instance they never call each other like 'dear' or 'honey' or 'baby'. I mean, I don't know any other couples enough to be an authority on this, but aren't they supposed to call each other that in this country? All the Hollywood movies I've seen as I grew up they almost always did. Bacall and Bogart, Hepburn and—I don't remember who her opposite was—They all seemed to call each other that, and made me look forward to having 'adult' relationships once I became a certain age. I thought it was so classy. (As for my parents, my mother would call my father 'dear' or 'Father', but my father would call my mother 'hey' or 'look here', like she didn't have any name and didn't deserve it. As long as he'd provide her—a terrible consequence of a match-making marriage.)

But Kira and Stephen, they always called each other by name. Kira was Kira, and Stephen was Stephen. At least in front of me. I always suspected it was because they had a business together. They were a married couple but at the same time they were business partners. You can't be lovee-dovee at each other when you are dealing with someone on the business level, I suppose. (That reminds me of all these wife and husband teams that owned businesses in my neighborhood in Japan: Either they would be very open about their relationships, so any goings on between them must be shared with customers or they acted like they didn't notice each other's being there.)

I guess Kira and Stephen's case is more or less the same. For me they are like a brother and sister. When they fight, each of them is determined not to be the first one to give up and make a step for reconciliation—Although these days Stephen seems becoming a lot more matured, and gives in just have a peace of mind. (Fighting with Kira must be exhausting, since belligerency is her second nature.) Like the other night, in a cab, on our way to the theater, he attempted to bring up some conversation which Kira didn't lend her ears. Consequently I was put to the position of having to acknowledge Stephen while pretending I wasn't aware they were at war. I knew it'd flip out Stephen, for he didn't want to the world to know what went between them. In a way it's very Stephen. But I understand. With the business they got they couldn't be enjoying the fight to bring them together closer—as some people say. Only Kira doesn't seem to give a damn.

14

I remember the day I met my sister for the first time. It's kind of odd to think there exists such a moment when you *meet* your very close relative. You'd think your core family member is something that creep in into your life; they were there before you knew it. For I've never exactly met my mother; I had been inside of her and came out there one day; and the father—I may have been introduced to him by a doctor or nurse but I can't remember how it went, naturally.

But I can recall the day my sister entered my life.

One evening, my grandaunt whom I'd been staying with during my mother's labor took me to the hospital. It was late fall, and when we went out of the house, the sky spread in somber pallid blue that made the street look dark and dismal. Beyond the anarchic array of powerlines fluttered bats. (How Tokyo has changed!)

We entered a stark corridor where unfriendly smell of chemicals greeted us to let us know it wasn't a pleasent place; its sinister message was apparent even to a three-year-old girl. Or it maybe when you are that small, you are more susceptible to those things.

We walked on in this sealed cylindrical space, without seeing any outside space, not even a night sky. Only the doors lined up on both walls with a steadiness of metronome: I'd walk fourteen steps and there'd a door, another fourteen steps, and another door, so went on.

I followed my grandaunt's hand-knit brown cardigan till she stopped in front of a door. She opened it, greeted whomever inside with her usual brusque manner, and pushed me in.

It was a grey room, grey as a wet naked concrete slab. (As I look back now, it's very unlikely for a hospital to have grey rooms, so the color must've been plastered up by my head.)

There were several people in the room, all standing around the bed. I think my father was one of them, but anybody else I didn't recognize.

"Oh, Satomi, you're here."

Mother said, as she lifted her head slightly from lying position. She looked different. She wasn't the mother I knew: she had pale puffy face and greasy hair—I looked closely around her cheek-to-neck area to see if I could find an evidence of a mask put on.

I couldn't move.

"Whadda ya doin', bein' so queer? C'mon, say 'ello to your mom."

Grandaunt pulled my arm.

I moved closer to bed cautiously, just in case my so-called mother would bare her trueself.

But it *was* my mother. Only she looked a little sickly. I felt sorry for her but at the same time so happy to see her.

'Mama', as I was going to call her name, she put her

arms softly around a thing that had been lying next to her and said,

"Satomi, it's your sister."

I stared it hard. It was apparently some flesh, as red as boiled octopus, and as wrinkled as a rotten apple. It was appalling. And it twitched! I jumped back.

"What's up, Satomi?"

My mother asked ever so tenderly for the first time that day, flashing her big right fang that's shiny as a pearl—her smile.

I could tell she was getting so much joy from this 'thing', so I wanted know about it, wanted share her happiness.

I examined it closely, trying to find a link between this 'thing' and the word 'sister'. The thing was not what I had pictured. I'd imagined my baby sister as lovely, cuddly, doll-like thing I could give milk to.

I glared at it for a while. Then I started to notice its little features: it got a mouth, nose and slits of eyes. It *was* a baby.

"Oh, she sleeps well . . . so adorable . . . "

Grandaunt let out a sigh of admiration. Then she turned to me,

"She looks so much like you, Satomi."

NO——!!

I was flabbergasted. This red wrinkly babything looks like me?! No way——!

Then my father rested his hand on my shoulder and said,

"You're a big sister from today."

'Rie' became her name. Not in Chinese characters, just in two alphabets. Ri-E. It sounds cute and spoiled—almost overfondly, but it has a modern ring to it, so I guess my parents succeeded in that regard. They apparently took great pain to name her, looking up various books on fortunetelling, and once they almost decided on 'Rie', they went to see a renowned numerologist for an advice, just to be certain. (Unlike the naming of 'Satomi': They named me after my late grandfather whose name was Satoshi. No research, no nothing, right on the spot!)

This was only the begining. Compared to me, everything was planned and well-cared for my sister. For instance when I was four or five, I was never allowed to have soft cream or any sweet when we went to the restaurant on the top floor of a department store on Sundays. But for my sister it was ritual. I remember her gobbling it wildly, fighting against its melting speed, trying not to miss any of drippings. (Because of her, I could also get to eat the cream, so may be I should thank her. . . .)

But the thing I detested the most was that I was deprived of any girly things—girly colors. Whenever we needed anything, a blanket, pen case, dresses, my mother would buy same two things in different colors, one for me one for Rie. Pink became her color and boy's color blue became mine.

15

"GWAaaa . . . !!"

Kazuko came rushing into the restaurant, completely out of breath. Her shoulders went up and down rapidly, like a reptilian respiration. She collapsed in a chair.

"Y . . . Yuya, sorry, but could you give me some water?"

She said, still gasping for air, and laid her face down on a table.

Erika and I looked at each other, brooms in our hand.

"Kazuko-san, here, water."

Yuya offered a glass, but she didn't raise her head.

"I'll, I'LL KILL HER!"

She banged the table hard. That seemed brought her back to her senses, she looked around to see if Mr. Ikeda was there. He was very fastidious about all of his business equipments, kitchen supplies, tables and chairs.

"Don't worry, he's not here yet."

Erika assured.

"But what on earth happened to you?"

Kazuko looked at all three of us with dejected eyes, took the glass off from Yuya, gulped it all down and started to talk.

* * *

This is what she told us:

Kazuko was waiting in a line for a cashier in a drugstore. There were three registers but only one was open. The line moved very slow, maybe because the cashier girl was new to the job, Kazuko thought. There was another girl who was standing next to the cashier girl, with a price sticker gun in her hand, who was may be teaching the girl ABC of cashiering, or may be just loitering—Kazuko couldn't tell.

After a few minutes in the line (it may have been less, may have been more—certainly felt more to Kazuko), Kazuko got to be the second person in line. Then all of a sudden, out of nowhere this big black woman who was in her forties dressed in a hospital-like uniform, cut in. She was merrily singing some gospel.

'WoW,' Kazuko thought, 'is she serious?'. The line behind her was still as long as when she started. 'That's not right.' So when her supposed turn came, she said to the black woman,

"Excuse me, but I was here before you," and dumped the merchandise in front of the cashier.

"You were?"

Kazuko couldn't tell if she'd said that or 'you what?'. The black woman raised her brow in exaggeration (to intimidate Kazuko).

"This girl here says she's here before me? Heh!"

She said to the cashier girl, and turned her sneer to Kazuko and said,

"You—likes of you should take a boat back to wherever you come from."

"——!"

This infuriated Kazuko. She felt blood boiling up. 'What

have I done? I've done nothing! It's this woman, who forces herself in!' She looked around quickly to see if anyone would back her up. She didn't put the cashier girl on a spot, so she turned around to see people in line, but met only a dozen of languid eyes. They, too, wanted just pay and get out. At the speed of light she thought about what to say—she knew one thing to say to get back at her, but she left it out. The fact that she couldn't say what she wanted say, or should be said, infuriated her even more.

"What do you mean by that? I live here. I pay tax ('to support *your* relative'—Kazuko didn't say), not like ('those guys deliver noodles on bicycle'—this, too, she didn't) . . . ('Didn't your lord tell you to love everybody?'—nor this), I'm a citizen here (here she bluffed), What are you gonna do about it?"

The woman glared at her as if she could spit with her eyes.

Tut! She clicked the tongue once and turned to the cashier girl, now started ignore Kazuko.

By this time Kazuko had goods bagged and got the change back, so she headed for the door though still not being able to suppress the bitter vexatious taste in the mouth. As she stormed out the store she heard the woman entertaining people around her by mocking Kazuko. She walked fast. Then faster. She wanted to shake off this aggravating incident, get rid of it like a pair of stained panties. She sped up, and up, until she was running.

". . . .So I came here to tell SOMEBODY about it. It's so horrible. To keep it inside of me. . . . I couldn't face my ancestors just yet, you know?"

She topped off her story with her religious inclination.

"It's so aggravating, that woman!"

Erika shrieked.

"Unforgivable!"

She was totally taken in.

Yuya and I were silent. I couldn't find what else to say other than inveigh against that woman. After Erika did it for me, I was left feeling weary of everything. Incidents like that would never go away. Either you tolerate them or go to live some place else where you'd be on the side to discriminate, instead of being discriminated. Then I felt guilty for thinking so negatively passive.

". . . There are so many of them. They presume we Asians don't talk back, which makes us the best target for their outlet—their oppressed feeling in general. . . ."

I started but wasn't sure what I wanted say myself.

"But we didn't put them where they are, did we? They've been treated badly ever since the beginning of time—I mean, beginning of this country. They are barking up the wrong tree. They can't take it out on me!"

Kazuko said, still fuming, you could see it down to the tip of her frizzy hair.

We fell in silent until Erika said,

"But it's not just blacks who try to pick on us. Till now I've completely forgotten but, a couple weeks ago when I was in a supermarket, getting cat food, it happened. This guy, in your typical faded shirt, didn't look exactly like a 'successful'person, probably has been living this area since when the rent was dirt cheap, taking catfood cans off a shelf. His cart was blocking the aisle, so I parked mine in front of him, or behind him, since he was facing the shelf.

Anyway, I got to the shelf, took some cans, and came back to my cart. By this point he was ready to move his cart away, but he couldn't because mine was in his way. There was no room for two carts to go by. So I hurried to push mine out of his way, and then he said, 'excuse me'. I said, 'sure', thinking he meant his cart'd been blocking the aisle. Then he went, 'I thought you're supposed to say that, Miss!'. You know, for me, it takes time to proccess English, so a few seconds later I understood what he'd said, and went, 'jerk!'. I know, you could say 'it's not racial, it could've happened to anyone', but the way he said 'Miss' wasn't very kind, like he was being sarcastic, 'you piece of shit doesn't deserve to be called that!'. . . . I wish I had said something back. It leaves real bad taste in your mouth, doesn't it—that you can't retort?"

"But, you gotta be careful, you could get stabbed or shot when you say a wrong thing."

Yuya said, concerned.

"That's it! You know, at the drugstore, what I really wanted say to her was 'why don't *you* go back to Africa?'. The words came to the tip of my tongue, real close, but I was surrounded by swarms of dark people, so I chickened out. I don't want to be beat up for a silly thing like that! Besides I didn't want to be taken as a racist just because this woman who *happened* to be black insulted me, hey, I lived with a brother a few times!"

Nobody said a thing for a few seconds. We sighed in unanimous silence.

Then to lift everybody's sprit, Yuya made fun of Kazuko.

" So Kazuko-san, you ran like a resurrected *Onibaba* to get away from the scene?"

"What? Did I look that terrible?"

Kazuko got the drift and pretended to show some concern by stroking her perpetually sunburnt face.

"Well, yeah, hair all flying, the face stiff as a frozen oyster—Didn't you think so?"

Yuya asked Erika and me for an agreement. In place of nod, we laughed.

"I see! OooKei . . . Yuya, girls don't care for a guy with a big mouth, you know that."

Kazuko snickered, using her age as a weapon: an advice from a matured and experienced.

"You don't have to worry about that."

"Oh, is that right?"

Kazuko raised her brows.

"Heh-heh-heh."

"Who's this girl?"

"Never mind. Tee-hee."

Yuya giggled coyly.

Erika obseved him, pouting.

"By the way Kazuko-san, aren't you due in at seven tonight?"

Erika asked.

"Yeah, I am. Right, you guys go back to what you're doing. I'm gonna kill some time and come back later."

She gathered up her stuff and got up.

The long afternoon sun was finally going down behind the city. The shadows from the building across the street was just about reach the glassed wall of this place. I had a feeling it was going to be a busy night.

As I finished wiping tables, Juan, our bus boy, came in.

"*Ohayo*, good evening, *buenas tardes*."

Yuya greeted him.

Juan smiled his Indian smile and raised his hand. He hardly spoke at work.

"Hey, Juan, can you move these sake barrels to the corner? They are way too heavy for me."

Yuya said.

It was a few years ago.

I came home depressed one day. In the street this guy had come up to me and asked.

"Are you Japanese?"

I was dubious about his abruptness, but answered,

"Yes?"

"I thought so."

Then he walked away. What was it all about? Did he make a bet with someone about my nationality? He walked pass me alone, and didn't seem to be joining anybody. It didn't make sense. After a while I felt that the guy had made a fool of me. I was ridiculed. But what for? For what reason? I didn't understand. I tried to reason: Maybe he was a psychic testing his ability—I tried to be positive. But the way the whole thing went didn't suggest that possibility: if he had been a psychic and could read my destiny, he would have pursueded me for a proper session.

O.K., I'm a Japanese and I look like it. But why does he have to remind me? Do I walk funny or something? I felt self-conscious. And miserable. The whole thing was too degrading.

When Kevin came home I told him about the incident and the way I felt—it was a discrimination.

He listened me intently, with an attitude of not to jump to conclusion, which was always the best part of him. After he heard me talk he said,

"I think you're making a mountain out of mole hill. I don't think he meant anything mean. He may simply wanted to know if you are Japanese and asked you."

"But if he did, he should have give me a reason or explanation of why he wanted to know. He must've known that leaving without giving any excuse would be terribly rude."

"Not necessarily so. People ask questions casually in the street. To know the time for instance."

"But when you ask someone the time, and they tell you, don't you say 'thank you' or something?—Actually it's not always done here, I find. . . ."

"See? Now you pick on this country but you don't mean a big thing, do you?"

Kevin said, feeling confident he was convincing me.

"No . . . I know."

I started to dread for this conversation was not going to go anywhere. Only if he had said, 'gee, it must have been terrible. I'm sorry. Let's go to bed', I would have been feeling better already.

"You know, when I was a kid I had a long narrow face, so kids teased me by calling me 'horsy'. Then when I was a teenager, I got teased for having a 'donkey dick'. In a phys-ed class, especially. 'Hey, D.D., what are you feeding yourself with?' It was awful. Made you want to kill them all by shoving their stinky sneaks in their braced mouth. But you know, everybody goes through that. . . .

He looked at me as if to ask me 'am I right?'.

I remained silent for a while then said,

"I guess you're right."

That night, laying down next to him, listening to his healthy steady breathing, I stared at the darkness, thinking:

They are not even in a same dimension—his experience and mine. Not even remotely. How I felt today is something he'll never ever understand.

16

For worrying too much not to be late by any means, I got to the airport a good hour early. The waiting area was crowded with swarms of people despite its stale air. The air-conditioner must not have been working well, and stickiness from the people and weather was getting worse every minute.

"It's gonna pour, I know it."

A young Puerto Rican mother, who held the hand of a little girl muttered to herself. The girl had probably her best outfit—cream-colored dress with layers and layers of white lace.

I looked up the sky. Outside the terminal, beyond the parking lot was pitch dark. Dark as a mole on the old guy's hand who was sitting on the formica chair against window, still as a turtle. He clutched on a well-used cane as if to balance himself from falling. He didn't look like he was waiting for anyone, rather he'd spend too much time waiting, he'd forgotten who or what he was waiting for.

The wind must be getting strong. I saw a couple of women crossing the parking lot, holding down at their skirts that wanted to blew open like an umbrella a la Marilyn. It'd be a real drag if it really rained, I thought.

I looked up on the TV screen for 'arrivals' for the fifth time to see if my sister's flight was still on time—it said it was. That meant I still had half an hour. Half an hour—thirty minutes—one thousand eight hundred seconds (is it?). I wasn't sure whether I was supposed to feel *still* half an hour, or *only* half an hour.

On my way here on the subway, I was sort of disappointed in myself for not being very emotional. For a person who was to see her sister for the first time in three years, for Chrissake, I found myself too dispassionate. Sure, it'd be nice to see her and all, but it wasn't like I couldn't control my horses thinking about it. It was almost, the most exciting part was listening to her telling me about her prospective visit over the phone. I'm not a very excitable person to start with, but even to see my sister—my blood sister? I felt I was some kind of coldhearted monster that didn't give a damn about anything or anyone. . . .

But now, I started worry. She'd be landing soon. Would I recognize her? Would she? Do I look all right? What would she think about my place? Hope she's not expecting a hotel quality—all that anxiety started to hit me all at once.

Among Latinos, came out Japanese looking bunch through the arriving door. I got closer to the pipe railings, as much as I could. More Japanese, Latino, Latino, Japanese. The flight from South America and Japan must have arrived at the same time.

With no time the area turned into a chaos. Families and

friends kissing and hugging each other in the midst of baggage carts, cardboard boxes and baby buggies. It was like a street party without plates of food. Only this was more emotional. Couples held each other tight, babies and kids smiled with glitters in their eyes, grandmas and grandpas wetted their eyes. Solely Japanese kept their bodies distance, bowed each other politely. I waited, keeping my eyes glued at the door. After about sixty, seventy people came out through the door (how many people exactly can a plane carry?), I saw a slender girl with apprehensive look on her face. It was Rie.

"Rie! Here I am!"

I thrust people aside with my shoulders and elbows to make a passage.

"Rie!"

She saw me and answered my waving with a relaxed smile.

"You've arrived."

I couldn't keep my eyes off her: I didn't remember her being this—luminous.

"Yeah. Here I am, alive and arrived!"

Rie proclaimed and giggled with her right shoulder slightly raised—a habit of her which I'd forgotten till now. I had a furious urge to hold her.

"Welcome to New York."

But I stood stiff, let my arms dangling uselessly, like an out-of-order payphone.

I cursed under my tongue at the so-called customary differences between this country and where I'm from, and above all, at my shyness, drowning in the roaring sea of hugs and kisses.

17

"Wow."

As soon as I opened the door Rie said, undoubtedly stunned.

"It . . . It's awesome."

"What do you mean?—Wait, don't put the suitcase in yet."

I walked by her side and took out a relatively fair looking rag from under the sink, and handed it to her.

"Wipe the bottom, will you?"

While we were on our way from the airport, it rained. It was a typical summer shower, heavy but brief, that left the street all shiny. We were in a high spirit; breathing cooled down late afternoon air, looking at the city that just had been washed crisp. Especially for Rie, it must've been a wonderful welcome. We rolled her suitcase from a subway station, pointing at this and that, laughing at them.

"Well, may I come in now?"

"Sure."

Rie lifted up the suitcase an inch from the floor to pass it over the doorsill.

"Hmm. . . . ."

She looked around the room curiously.

"There's nothing to write home about, is there?"

I pressed her before she had time to comment, as a manner of self-defence.

To put it bluntly, it wasn't even *my* apartment. I was only subletting it for a year. A tiny space crammed with sink, stove and refridge—A futon, TV-audio, and clothes were pretty much only thing I brought.

"What's that? Could it be a—shower?"

She went up to the strange looking apparatus in the corner of the room.

"You guessed it right."

It was indeed a shower, a homemade kind. It basicaly consisted of big plastic wash basin, covered with horrible puke-y green vinyl cloth that being hung from the ceiling. Something about it made me think of the metal coffins that they keep the frozen bodics to be revived in the future. This one was low budget B-movie version of it though.

"It's up to you to call this thing a shower, but it serves its purpose," I said.

It was true. I was lucky enough to have something like this apartment, no matter how terribly rundown. While I was looking for a place to move in, I became almost certain that I had to go to Brooklyn, and I was dreading that idea. Small, but an *apartment*, not a *room*, all by yourself, in Manhattan—For that I'd even tolerate a communal toilet in the hall.

"Why don't you sit down. I'll make you some tea."

I pointed at the only chair in the place.

"Umm. . . ."

She half hesitantly took a seat and shifted her eyes around further more, gingerly, as if to fill a gap between what she'd pictured and what she was seeing. I guess it couldn't be helped.

"You said this place is sublet, but what is it, exactly?"

So I explained what it is and incidently told her about the person I subletted the place from.

—Though I'd never met him, the rumor had it that he was an elite Japanese businessman. When a guy, who was an acquintance of his and a sushi chef at the restaurant I used to work, told me about the place, I couldn't link the two together. Why does a successful businessman live in such a low rent place (for him particularly) in way-East Village? I'd always thought a Japanese businessman lived in a suburb if he had a family (just like the case of Mihoko's husband), or in a high rise condo in Midtown if he was single. So at first I rationalized the mystery by thinking that he may be living in a old but well-kept place in East Village for its convenience—there are a lot of Japanese restaurants and grocery stores that sell Japanese products; you can even get a *bento* box to go, which is kind of homey for a Japanese guy sometimes. And I didn't stop it there. I started think he may wanted to have somebody live in his place while he was away (he was being sent to London) for an upkeep in general and for a sort of burglar-proof. But of course I was wrong. All the way, way off. When I opened door to the place the whole thing turned out to be my wishful thinking, a daydream—so unlikely of me.

The place was genuine dire. The wall paper bulged and

sagged in places; there was a ghoulish stain on the ceiling that looked like a face of a nasty clown; the floor wood was so old you'd most certainly prick yourself if you tried to walk in barefoot; then there was this window that had not been cleaned at least ten years, blocking already scant sunlight with its curtain of filth. It'd have been totally terrifing if the place was in a complete mess. But that wasn't the case. (I mean, the condition of the apartment itself was a mess, but the attitude of occupant wasn't. He paid his best effort to keep it tidy.)

I could see this guy had very few belongings. The room was as bare as if he'd already moved out of the place. There was no likely furniture such as a couch or bed. A school auditorium type of folding chair and a table sat near the kitchen, and against one wall stood rolled up (abominably) darkened gym mat, which I assumed he must have slept on. No TV, not even a cassette player, not a book nor magazine was lying around. The barely visible sign of life was a bag of dried mushroom which was tucked in a kitchen shelf between a few spices. A very conservative kind of suit and some shirts hung on the clothes bar. It was a little creepy. An elite businessman's residence? What I'd heard didn't make much sense but I decided to take the place nonetheless.

Later that day when I told the sushi chef my plan, I asked him to tell me a little more about the guy, that I was ready to hear anything, even if he'd killed his girlfriend in the apartment and got off the charge I'd still move in to the place.

"Don't tell anybody, O.K.?," he said, lowering his voice and looked out around him left and right,

"He apparently belongs to some religious cult, and said to be giving away all his earnings to them. I don't know exactly how much he makes but you can imagine."

"Does that mean some people from the cult could come and visit me sometime?"

I wasn't thrilled about the idea. Not at all.

"No, I don't think so. The lease is signed under his name as far as I know, so I don't see how anybody could come and take over. I know someone who subletted his place for a few month while ago, but everything turned out fine. In a sense, the money you pay him goes to the cult anyway. . . . . Besides, if you're not afraid of ghosts, why would you be afraid of a living soul?"

HA-HA-HA, he made a crunchy laugh.

Heh-heh-heh, I followed him quizically.

"So, that shirt belongs to *him*?"

Rie asked, pointing at a used-to-be-pink-now-you-don't-know colored golf shirt on the clothe bar.

"Yep."

"Oh, I feel much better. You know, I was wondering if it belonged to your boyfriend. And if it did, I may be putting his life into jeopardy by coming to stay here."

"Oh, no, don't worry about that. There's no such person in my life right now, unfortunately."

I said. Even if there was, he wouldn't be wearing that shirt, I thought. Even I would draw a line somewhere. I couldn't be that desperate.

18

For her first night in New York, I took Rie to a Spanish restaurant on Tenth Street. It was her suggestion, not mine, to go Spanish. Since she'd been on the plane for so many hours, I asked her,

"Are you sure you can handle oil and all? Don't you wanna eat something a little more easy on you?"

But she shook her head in determination, seemingly her mind set,

"No, I'm fine. Unless you feel that way, we could go elsewhere."

"I'll go for anything. It's your first night."

"All right, then. Spanish it is."

Then she told me that Spanish food was IN for big time in Japan. So were Spaniards. I could almost picture a leading article in a women's magazine:

"I WANT TO BE SUCKED LIKE A KALAMATA OLIVE!" —THE CONFESSION OF JAPANESE *MALINCHE*!!

There seemed to be a craze for guys of a particular racial-cultural background every few years. Around the time I left Japan, it was black guys. Before that was Italians. Next year could be Lithuanians, who knows.

I told her about the place on Tenth Street I'd been with Kira, that they had great tapas but didn't serve paella.

"A *real* tapas bar, then."

She got excited and explained to me that tapas bars must not have paella on the menu.

"When people say paella they usually mean the rice dish with chicken and seafood mixed in. But that's just one of many kinds of paella—Valencia style. Like we have many different types of ramen noodles, the same goes with paella. Practically every region has its own. For instance in Barcelona they have one with rabbit; then if you go north of there to greater Catalonia, the typical one is just with vegetables. The word 'paella' means the shallow pan they cook the dish in, and its size, the diameter, must match the size of the flame. Some places people eat out of pan directly with a fork, without plates."

"Hmm. . . . ," I sighed, deeply impressed.

"Where did you learn all this? Did you go on a 'In search of paella's roots' tour or something?"

"Oh, I've read about it in a magazine."

I guess in Japan there's enough information to kill a business or two for lacking the authenticity.

Over dinner I watched Rie use a knife and fork skillfully. While holding the meat down with a fork, you press and pull a knife toward you, without pushing out the elbows—She was doing it gracefully. Where has she learned this? In a magazine? Can't be. It'd require practice.

In our family, we never ate with a knife and fork except one day out of a whole year—Christmas Eve. On that day our mother would make corn soup and salad, put roasted chicken legs from a deli on a plate and we would eat all the dishes simultaneously (!) with a knife and fork, while we watched television. The rest three hundred and sixty four days, we, three of us, mother, Rie and me, sat in the kitchen and ate with chopsticks, save for curry, which we ate with a spoon. (Our father never ate with us: he'd come home after we'd eaten, start drinking sake first, and eventually have dinner.)

It's such a strange feeling to witness someone, who you thought knew very well, who shared the ritual for so many years, display the part—advanced—you never knew. Twenty some years since her birth I'd known her, but then, last eight years I only saw her a few days here and there. The very last time was three years ago, but I didn't remember if I'd felt like this. She seemed to have—I don't know the proper expression—grown since then, more sophisticated and womanly.

"Umm. . . .These sardines are marvoulous. Have you had some? You gotta have it," Rie said.

"Yeah, sure. . . .but wait, you never used to like sardines. You always cried when you were forced to eat them."

"I know. It wasn't at the level of 'I *didn't like* them'. I *hated* them, they absolutely disgusted me. But now I love them. I'd eat any blue fish that I couldn't eat before. It's interesting, isn't, with the age your tastebuds change. . . .As for sardines, I hesitate to say but, it was a lot to do with the way Mother prepared them. You can't just plain-grill sardines, you need some oil, spices. . . ."

Rie recounted, while contently putting the fish into the mouth.

"Do you cook a lot at home for Masahiko?"

Masahiko is a guy Rie has been living together for a few months.

"Sure I do. Not everyday though. Sometimes I get pre-packed ready-to-eat stuff from a *conbini* store and serve, but he doesn't object, thank God. He seems to be happy as long as he can eat something in his pajamas, without going out."

She giggled as if she was hinting the profusely amorous time they were having together, sort of like *In the Realm Of the Senses.*

"Thanks for sharing your happiness. But frankly, I'm quite stunned to hear that coming from my little sister's mouth."

" Oh, no! I don't mean sexual stuff. . . . ."

She blushed lightly.

Same old her, same new her. The two took turns, moving up and down like a merry-go-round. I smiled.

"Still, he wasn't reluctant to let you go three long weeks?"

"No, didn't even bat an eye. He knows I haven't had any serious time off from work for last few years, and once we—our office gets going I won't have time . . . Moreover, once I decided to come here I campaigned the trip as 'heartwarming sisters reunion tour'. He was all in for it."

She snickered.

"You mean you didn't just come see me?"

I said, and made a hurt face.

"Oh, Sis—"

She was in a flurry. I stuck out my tongue.

"Just kidding!"

"You!"

She went through the motion of throwing the napkin at me. We had a hearty laugh.

19

"You still have this record?"

Rie asked, in the tone that was neither praise nor disapproval. Or it could've been both.

"Sure thing."

I said as I eyed on The Smiths' album Rie pulled out of the shelf.

Their very first one. I used to spin it over and over, day and night. I could still sing some of the songs.

I was happy in the daze of drunken hour
but heaven knows I'm miserable now

I was looking for a job then I found a job
but heaven knows I'm miserable now

In my life
why do I give valuable time
to people who don't care if I live or die. . . .

I loved Morrissey's shy, boys choir kind of voice(the boy too shy to even join the choir). It flowed like a stream that soothed the nape of the reeds, turning occasionaly into a rapids that carried the silts all the way down the river. If every generation needs its cultural icon, Dylan for the sixties, and The Stones after that, The Smiths was it for me.

Rie studied the album cover, fingering the each side of it, lost in thoughts. Then after a while she looked up to me as if she had enough of introspection.

"I have something for you."

She took out a manila envelope from her back pack and handed it to me.

"From Mother."

The moment before she even said that I recognized the handwriting on the envelope. 'To Miss. Satomi', it said.

I opened and fished out what was inside: Brand new ten thousand yen notes—about thirty of them—and a letter.

"I envy you for getting something like that, just because you live in a foreign land. . . . I don't even know how they came up with that kind of money."

Rie said half mockingly. It was true. In our household, while I was still in Japan, I never saw money of that amount being exchanged. I mean, there were bills to be paid, not to mention the tuitions for both Rie and me among the other big expenditure, but never in cash.

My heart wrenched with gratitude; the bridge of my nose ached for the trouble they must have gone through. I could barely restrain myself from bursting into tears.

The money was definitely going to help. I had no idea what I would do with it right away for the amount was dearly abstract.

I took a deep breath and pushed back the tears, then started reading the letter.

Dear Satomi,

I'm sure you're fine.

Since Rie is going to see you in New York, I took an opportunity to write to you. Pardon me for my terrible hand writing. I'm hoping to write you someday like my calligraphy teacher. 'Someday'got to be soon enough, before my days expires. According to my doctor I have good twenty years to go, but you know, you never know. (Sorry, I try not to think about stuff like this, but it's rainy out and I'm sitting here alone, thinking and worrying about Rie's going to New York for nearly a month—What if she too decided to stay there? What would I do? . . . I've been happy to have two daughters instead of two sons, like your father wanted. But where are they now? Nobody stays with me or visits me once a while?—You know, the thoughts just go on and on in my head. Though I know Rie is coming back; she finally seems to have found somebody—Mr. Kasai, I'm talking about. At the beginning I was very depressed , and still am a little skeptical about Rie's living with him—a guy with a separated wife and two children. I cannot help thinking it may be a bad karma; otherwise why must my daughter fall for a guy like that, instead of a regular single guy of her age, while the other daughter is far away? . . . But these days I try to tell myself that you're not kids, and I should be happy as long as you're healthy and happy—Are you? Are you happy?

I seem to ramble every chance I get these days, excuse me. . . .

But you know when you're busy you tend to neglect your health. So be careful and eat well. I hear it's going to be hot where you are. Make sure you don't get summer fatigue; garlic, chives, and beef or chicken liver are all good for preventing it.

I enclosed some money to be used in case of emergency. You don't know what might happen when you're in a foreign country. Don't pay for a dead horse, needless to say.

Well then, now I'll rest my pen. Be good and well.

Yours sincerely,

Mother

P.S. (I'm most reluctant to mention it but)Don't you feel like coming home even a little while? Mrs. Takeda (my calligraphy teacher) says she maybe able to find a job for you. At your age, you may want to think seriously about your future. Think it over a little, would you?

I heaved a deep sigh. Feeling not being able to talk for a while, I took time folding the letter neat and put it back into the envelope. Mother definitely had a knack of making me miss home. Home, that's a big ocean and a continent away. I sighed again.

". . . Did she ask you to come home?"

Rie asked, choosing the right moment to pick up a conversation again.

"How did you know?—Does she say that a lot?"

The sense of guilt, which was once uncertain, started taking hold of its shape within me.

"Well, she spills it out time to time, that she wishes you

were there; she says she's tired of lying to her neighbors all the time."

I didn't miss her faint fidget(for slipping her tongue).

"What lie? That I live here in America?"

I demanded the explanation.

". . . .No, but she tells people you go to some prestigious language school."

"What!?"

I was stuuned. For what reason does she do that?, I nearly flew out at Rie. But I knew. I knew what it was at through and through. A terrible draining feeling came over me.

"Basically she's ashamed of me being at loose ends, right?

I gave it the form of question though I said it mainly for my self-awareness.

"Well. . . , you know she's from the generation who's been pounded on 'idling is an enemy', that as long as you're occupied doing something, it's good—even if you're not making a penny out of it. She fears some kind of retaliation from life later on if she's not being busy. I kind of understand her point, but when it gets to be too superstitious, I say it's nonsense, frankly. . . . Like she was against my going with Masahiko, not just because he had some tangle in his personal life, but because he was a freelancer. The fact that he can take a break at four in the afternoon to take a walk really bothers her, I think. To her, a proper job is nine-to-five or ten-to-six and the rest is just a plain B.S. . . . . She doesn't understand people work seriously, and sometimes longer hours at night too, you know?"

Rie said to humor me, and I appreciated that, but the

damage was done. The dagger got stuck. I started despise the stupid vanity of my mother's.

"Mother misses you. That's the bottom line. If she can see your face, nothing matters. I *know* that. . . .Don't you wanna think about going back there for even a few days, for a week? I think you'll have good time, seeing your old friends again and stuff. Then you can come back here. She'd probably pay your airfare if you wanted, on top of that three hundred thousand yen. . . . ."

'But I can't Rie!'——I wanted say out loud. My visa and passport had been expired long ago—if I left this country now I could never come back. I couldn't tell that to Rie or Mother, who was hyper-sensitive about being good—a law-abiding citizen. She'd go to pieces.

"Maybe sometime," I said.

"Yeah, you really should. Although she keeps herself busy with variety of lessons—calligraphy, flower arrangement, and swimming—she's lonely. You know how it is."

"Wait. What happened to her job?"

My mother worked in an assembly line at a subcontracter of huge electric company.

"Are you serious? She retired from it a couple years ago."

She looked at me in amazement.

"And Father, then?"

"He's in semi-retirement. He retired from the headquarters but goes around trade high schools to recruit future personnel for the Self Defense Army."

"You mean he gives speeches and all?"

"Yeah, all over Japan, apparently."

"Our father? That 'lion at home and mouse abroad', giving speeches?"

"Yep . . . but it won't be long till he settles at home. . . ."

"Hmmm. . . . . . . "

I pictured my mother and father sitting in their house all alone. The two lonely people whose loneliness have never merged under one roof.

20

Eight years is a long time. Though when you're in the midst of living it it doesn't seem to add up much. Today, tomorrow. Today, tomorrow. It goes like that like a marching band. Steady most of the time, slows down at the intersection time to time.

But when you stand still and look back you'd be amazed by its volume. Where has all this time gone? You have no chance to run into it again, not like your old boyfriends or girlfriends—it's vanished. Forever. Gone. Gone. Gone.

In eight years a new born baby becomes a third grader, a high school girl becomes an office girl, or possibly a housewife.

In eight years the presidential election came around twice, so did the leap years. (Why is a 'leap year' called 'leap year'? It doesn't skip ahead, it adds a day.)

Eight years—it's almost one third of my life. It's a scary thought but that's the fact. And I've done nothing. I didn't discover the miraculous cure for an epidemic, didn't invest in micro world, didn't fight in a war. I've done nothing that matters to anybody, let alone the world.

'Are you happy?', my mother asked. Am I? I refuse to answer, refused to even think about it.

* * *

Sometimes I can't help wondering about what would have happened if I had stayed in Japan. Found a job in some small printing company in northern part of Tokyo, pouring teas and doing some errands? Or turned my back to a career and found an employment in an entertainment—night club hostess business? Or I could be married with two children.

No matter what kind of life I'd been leading, if I was there I feel I could manage it pretty well with a occasional grumble. Betting on a horse race once in a while, singing Karaoke once in a while.

I'd probably be satisfied with my life to certain extent, and moreover, probably wouldn't have a chance or desire to look back on the past as often as I do. I'd read the magazines, be informed to follow trends, and let the flow take me wherever. . . . . .

Only here the life seems marginal.

'The real expression is to scrape the scorch off the bottom of your conscious,' someone said.

In that case I'm only scooping the lye.

Lacking the drive is my biggest curse. I've been interested in anything and everything, but I never had my calling. I've never felt an urge to do anything. I've never lost my sleep over anything except relationship trouble or worries in general. I've never feverishly tackled with a thing that I got carried away and lost the sense of time. . . .

I've painted some paintings, wrote a few poems, sang some songs, but that was that. It was like a fit every time. I'd go through a few stormy days or weeks, then all at once throw everything away. I'd literally dump every stuff I worked on up till that point away—I can't be reminded of a failure—I *have to* move on to a new thing. As if searching for a tiny clue that could open the door to my untapped existance, I move on, one from the other.

I'm an artist in my mind alone: I'm a blind painter, stammering poet and bathroom crooner.

That's all I am.

21

I called Kira five times in three days, but got no answer. Just the usual answering machine playing Bukka White's 'Where can I change my clothes'. I guess it's a some kind of joke, though not exactly in good taste. She left the machine on all the time whether she was in or not, so it is possible she wasn't in a 'pick up the phone' mood and just let her machine do what it's supposed to do.

I was almost giving up calling her, thinking she may be out of town, though she'd never told me. But you never know with her. It was my sixth call that finally caught her attention. She came to the phone sounding half-asleep and tongue heavy.

"He . . lo . . . , Satomi?"

"Kira! Where've you been? I've been calling you for days. What's up?"

"W . . e . . ll, n . . . nothing new. Heh, heh."

She said with a slight slurr and it alarmed me: 'heh heh' is not like her either.

"Are you watching TV or something?"

"Uh-uh. . . ."

That was all she said.

"Are you O.K. there?"

"Oh, fine, fine."

"You sound like you had some drink."

"No, I'm not I. . . ."

I waited her to continue but a few seconds passed in silence.

"He—llo! Yoo-hoo! Earth to Kira?"

"Oh, sorry, what? Where was I?

"I asked if you had some drink, in other words if you're drunk, and you said no."

I was started to be annoyed.

"No, I'm not. I swear to God."

"To God?"

She never swear anything to God. She became his follower only when she needed something out of him.

"Yeah, I swear."

She said, taking my ? as a stress.

Why doesn't she admit she is drunk? If she wants to she can drink, I'm not her mother, I won't scold her—I thought. Unless she was on something else other than alcohol; still, in that case she was being honest. But as far as I knew she only smoked a few puffs very rarely.

"Kira, I can call you back later, or you can call me, whatever—"

"No! Don't hang up. I'm sorry, but stay on the line."

Her voice had a tinge of urgency.

"But. . . . ."

"What day is this?"

"Twenty-first."

"The day of the week?"

"Thursday."

"I see. . . ."

"Where were you? Were you on the moon?"

I almost couldn't tease her: I had an eerie feeling she may have been on the moon.

"Ah, I've been sleeping a lot . . . I may be under the weather from air-conditioning. . . ."

We fell in silence again. I listened to the sound of telephone—millions of cables that connected me to Kira.

"—Satomi, are you there?"

"Yeah, I'm here."

I answered, not quite being able to conceal my irritation.

"Which do you prefer, to live happily in falseness or live miserably but in truth?"

She asked me out of nowhere.

"What kind of 'truth' are we talking about? 'I'm fat', 'I'm ugly' that kind of thing?"

"In this case, it is one's faith, belief . . . "

"And the false happy life? Do I know it's false? I'm in a falseness without knowing it?"

"Right, you don't know it's false. You are being deceived."

"Then I'd take a happy life."

"You would?"

She raised her voice, seemingly surprised.

"Yeah, why? The choice is obvious, isn't it?"

"I thought you'd say you prefer the life with truth."

"Well . . . ," I tried to give a matter a little more thought.

Happy but false, or pitiful but truthful—I'd still take a happy life. My life is miserable sometimes, not because I pursue the truth of living: It just is. If Kira somehow thought I was living a life to fulfill my purpose, she was dead wrong. Only bourgeois think 'in the depth of destitution, lies the mother-of-pearl-like meaning of life' sort of thing.

"False life, it is. Besides if you don't know you're being deceived till you're dead, then the falseness becomes truth to you, doesn't it?"

"But people who you know would pity you for living the life you lived after your death."

"I don't care whatever happens after I'm gone—Do you?"

"Well, actually I guess I don't."

Kira said.

"But what is this all about? The question? You're not referring to your own life, are you?"

"Oh, no. No. I saw it in a magazine and wondered what you'd say."

"What would you say?"

"Me? Oh, I don't know—That's why I asked you,—excuse me."

I heard her cough. It sounded pretty mean.

"Kira, you all right?"

"Oh, yeah. You know I'm finding out I have an allergy, after all these years."

"What sort?"

"Mac."

"Oh."

I felt sorry for the innocent little fur ball.

"Can you do anything about your allergy?"

"No. They say the best remedy is to stay away. But I can't do that, obviously. So I gotta live with it."

She cleared her throat. Another little silence.

"You know I called 'cause my sister got to town."

"Oh, she's here! How fantastic!"

Now she sounded more like her.

"So I thought maybe we can get together . . . "

"Sure, that'll be great. . . .Wait, what day did you say it was today?"

"Thursday."

"Well, how about Sunday? Dinner, perhaps?"

"Sounds good."

This time I said with ease, thanks to the money from my mother.

"Come around here five-ish. Though I'll speak to you before that."

"O.K.."

Then we hung up.

22

SoHo seemes to be changing forever. Whenever I walk through the neighborhood, usually to see Kira, I find some new business is going up there. It could be a restaurant, a bar, a store or a gallery. It's not rare to see the store I liked (not that I could afford to buy anything) for its oddness of being there, has gone the next time I pass by.

I seem to remember the first time I ever set my foot in the area I was let down. It didn't meet my expectations. Prior to my arrival in New York I absolutely devoured magazines, books, and travel guides to get as much information as possible. They all represented SoHo as 'the place for artists'—full of galleries and trendy cafes set in a 'creative atmosphere'. So I depicted in my mind of tree-lined streets dabbed with open-air cafes where 'artistic' types hang around to have zealous debate on anything that catches their fancy.

Although I had seen movies set in SoHo, such as *After Hours* and *9 ½ weeks*, which showed the actual streets of SoHo, I somehow managed to mis-project the image of another artistic place—Quartier Latin in sixties. I say sixties because I had dressed up a prototype of my scenester in a black turtle neck and a beret (!). He looked a lot like Crispin Glover—Didn't he play a character like that in a movie. . . .?

Basically I was off.

Yes, there were cafes, there were galleries, but former was taken up by yups and tourists, latter by 'cool'receptionsts. I didn't see any arty types—gloomy but excitable at the same time—kind of people at all. People there looked like they were all on the stage in their head. . . . Since then I made up my mind to take any written travel information lightly.

And so when Rie told me she'd gone to SoHo to browse I asked what she thought of the place. (I figured she must have read similar kind of blown-up articles.)

"Just about what I thought, no more, no less," she said matter-of-factly. I was a little disappointed with her answer, so I asked again specifically if she felt the gap between what she'd read and what she saw.

"Well . . . ," she took a little time and told me about her first trip abroad to the South-East Asia. She told me how her 'tour to a remote village' was disappointing, since it wasn't quite the way it was described in a brochure. She was supposed to (and expected to) meet charming village people, but ended up shaking off charming-to-get-a-buck villagers.

"I've learned the hard way. Those people who give you information are irresponsible. The pages are paid for by some tourists organization or another, so they'd jazz up anything to please the sponsors. . . . I mean, I guess the business I'm going into is closely tied with that kind of thing. . . . Anyway the point is 'when you don't expect much, you won't be betrayed as much'."

She was definitely my sister. After all these years spent

with the same parents, being grounded in the same principles over and over, we seemed to have nurtured the same phylosophy. 'Don't dream, don't hope, just follow the orders'. . . . .

Rie and I walked to Kira's from my place. Via Broadway to Prince and crossed over SoHo to Sixth Avenue. The streets were pretty busy, but it was a nice afternoon so we didn't mind. After a couple of wet days that made my place feel like tropical, we appreciated the clear sky and cool breeze. A perfect day for shopping—for a lot of people.

Rie wanted to stop by at Agnes B.to see if the summer top she had her eye on was still there. It was a nice salmon-colored cotton shirt. Very simple.

She held the shirt over her and stood in front of a mirror, with a concerned look on her face.

"It's a nice pink on you," I said.

"You think so?"

Rie turned around, happy to get someone's affirmation. Hey, that's what a sister is for, isn't it?

"O.K., I'll take it."

While she stood in a line at the cash register, I looked at the price tag.

"It's steep!"

I said out loud involuntarily.

For *a* shirt?

Then Rie looked at me and said,

"But think about getting the same piece in Japan!"

I got her point.

* * *

Kira came to the door holding Mac in her arms. Even with the suffering from the allergy, her love to him didn't seem to have changed.

"Welcome, Rie-chan, commin, come in."

Kira said in high spirit.

"WOW—! What a beautiful place!"

Rie exclaimed. This 'wow' seemed to be the common reaction to anyone who visited this place for the first time.

"WowWowWow—you can see all over SoHo! . . . Wow, I see SoHo is on a slope, isn't it?"

Rie shot her glittering eyes to Kira, full of admiration.

"Yes. I had no idea myself till I moved in here."

"SoHo is on a slope? What do you mean?"

I looked out intently at the rooftops to see what they were talking about.

They were right. When you looked closely, you could see the building tops near the eastern end of skyline stood in layers like stage props.

"I've never noticed it before."

I said, amazed by Rie's eyes.

"It's such a gorgeous place. . . .This feels like definitely New York."

Rie stood in a daze as if she was being hypnotized.

"Excuse me! Are you implying my place is not quite New York enough for you?"

I said it as a joke. Kira forced a smile,

"Oh, but your place is the other en. . . . .,"she paused briefly there,

". . . another area of Manhattan . . . East Village is also nice."

I was sure she had meant say 'other end of hemisphere' and realized.

"It's a bit guerilla war out there, but I like it . . . Though for me, for a typical tourist, SoHo seems to be the navel of New York."

Rie said.

"But you know a place like this—having a glassed roof and stuff—always creates a problem. Look"

Kira pointed at the discolored streak that ran down the wall. A minor water damage.

"It's a hassle."

She emphasized the pain to free herself from the guilty conscience (though I didn't know why she should feel like that), the same way she always told me her new designer dress was on sale.

"Still I wouldn't wanna live anywhere else if I had a place like this."

Rie said.

"I suppose so."

Kira admitted uncomfortably.

"Hmm. . . .,"

Kira looked at Rie and me by turns and said,

"You guys don't look much alike. I somehow expected Rie-chan was a smaller and younger version of Satomi, but you two don't seem to belong to the same type."

"What kind of type am I?"

I asked. I didn't like the idea of being typfied, particularly by Kira.

"What I mean is the impression of you from your look,

not what's inside, O.K.? For me you look diligent and prudent, a person who'd go right into a task of what you believe in, like Mme.Curie . . . But Rie is a little softer, more easy-going. . . ."

—And she's prettier and less shy and most of all cheerful, I thought. Because of these qualities, she was loved profusely by my parents.

"I have an eager-beaver part in me, too, not soft all the way . . . "

Rie smiled humbly, obviously liking what Kira said of her.

"How about you Kira? Do you have any sisters or brothers?"

"I have a younger brother I haven't seen for a couple of years. We aren't that close anyway, maybe because of the gender difference. I wish I had a sister, too."

"But if he's your brother he must be great-looking."

"Not only that, he's intelligent, too,"

I said,

"He's at Oxford, isn't he, Kira?"

I heard about this brother of Kira's who was in the graduate school, who Kira once described as 'a square bore'.

"Uh-huh."

She looked not altogether bad.

"Awesome! Maybe you could introduce me to him sometime."

Rie joked.

"Oh, you don't want that, do you?"

Kira winked as if to hint something,

". . . So tell me Rie, Satomi told me you're gonna be an illustrator?"

"Y . . . Yes."

She fidgeted a little, and at once shot a glance at me.

"I've been doing illustrations for small ads whenever I got an offer, while I kept my day job. But since it's been going well I decided to take a chance to pursue it full time."

"Good for you. Hmm. . . . Is your boyfriend an illustrator, too?"

Rie took a quick shot at me again, with an annoyed look.

"No, actually, he's a graphic designer. He draws some stuff but . . . "

Rie answered Kira cordially but I could feel her irritation was growing toward me.

"We know it's an adventure to start our own office, especially for me since I haven't got any experience. From an office girl to, all of a sudden, an illustrator—it's a plunge, I know. But as an office girl I saw I was in a fix, and I couldn't see myself doing the same job for year after year, so I made my decision."

"Oh, I really stand up for you. Really great. I guess when you're young anything is possible. . . ."

"No, don't say that. You're only a few years older than I am!"

Rie seemed a little embarrassed at Kira's flattering remark.

"Those few years make a big difference when you're pushing thirty. Don't they, Satomi?"

"Absolutely," I said.

After Kira went into the bedroom to give her hair final touch (it was a very peculiar thing about her: she never let you see her making herself up), Rie confronted me in a low voice.

"Why did you tell her so much about me?"

She asked. I didn't understand why she was so fuming.

"What's the big deal?"

"Did you tell her Masahiko was separated from his wife and two children? You did, didn't you?"

"Yeah—"

I admitted,

"But so what?"

"So what? How could you say such a thing? Why do you have to tell people that kind of fringy stuff? It's totally unnecessary. Yeah, I've been living with a man separated from his wife. But it only so happened that it's the guy I fell in love with."

"I know that but. . . . I tell you, as your sister, I wanted to talk the matter over with my friend."

"Talk? To do what? You guys are only gossiping like bored housewives, raising the curious eyes to my situation, just for an entertainment."

"That's not true. I really care for you."

I said and meant it. She became quiet for a while and said,

"Think about yourself being asked probing questions from somebody you never met before."

". . . But I thought you guys seem to be getting along very well."

"Yeah, I do like her but that's not the point."

"But she didn't ask every detail about your relationship with him."

"Oh, I know that. It's just I've been asked so much about this and that and, hearing 'oh, it's scandalous' or 'it's an adultery' that kind of nothing but out of curiosity two cents from the people I thought were my friends, including my parents. I'm getting fed up. . . .You can't blame me for being hyper-sensitive."

Kira hadn't told me (so typical), but it turned out that we were going to be taken out by Stephen. It seemed whenever Stephen was in town, Kira didn't want to go out by herself, particularly to dinner. I never asked if it was her doing or his—her hesitation to leave Stephen alone or his reluctance to let her go out alone (It was so unlikely of Stephen though). Anyhow this part remained vague to an unmarried . . . .

Stephen was going to take us to a new restaurant on Bowery, that got a lot of write-ups in various magazines since its opening a couple of months ago. So Kira's plan was to pick Stephen up from the store on Greene Street and walk over to the restaurant.

As we pushed the massive glass door, I saw Rie's eyes sparkled with a sheer excitement. We were in M-Mori, Stephen's store.

Once you were there, you'd be just amazed by its splendor—red antique damask from the ceiling, said-to-be twelfth-century tapestry of St.Ursula over one wall (once I asked Stephen about the authenticity of this piece, but he never gave me a straight answer), chairs, pillows, bedframes from different origins; Italy, Spain, Morocco, Afghanistan and China scattered around the room in curious concord.

It was kind of Zeffirelli's nightmare, Ken Russell's nursery—bizarreness so ravishing, it was spellbinding. The store made me feel closer to Stephen. On a personal level sometimes he was so aloof and gave me a hard time but seeing the store always had me gain back my respect for him—for his taste, and for what he put together.

While Rie and I stood in the middle of the room, happily lost in indulgence for the eyes, a very capable-looking wasp girl, who had her reddish hair pulled in a bun, came up to Kira.

"Hello, Kira."

"Hi," she said with a little nervous smile.

I saw Stephen coming from the back of the room.

"Kira," he said and kissed on her cheek courteously.

She didn't kiss him back, I saw her body somehow got stiffened: she kept looking straight like she was made of ice. Then she loosened her lips to crack a smile and introduced Stephen to Rie.

"Nice to meet you."

Rie looked feebly uneasy, facing the situation she must speak English.

"Beautiful store."

Rie said and smiled.

"Thank you."

Stephen said and smiled.

Kira started to make rounds as if she hadn't been to this place in a while. She picked up pillows and examined them, touched a drapery, turned a floor lamp on and off. The girl with a bun followed after Kira and gave her a description of each piece. Kira nodded at her and looked at the place in detached tenderness.

"Shall we go?"

Stephen looked around us for an agreement.
"Kira, are you ready?"
He called out.
"Yeah, I am"
She replied and walked slowly toward us.
"—Not for everything, but for dinner, I'm ready."
Kira said with an air of obnoxious child. Stephen frowned. I wondered what it was all about.

At a glance, you could see the restaurant was happening place. Fashionable-looking people crammed in the soft amber lit room. It made me think of the thirties—the way everything shone, the way diamantes dazzled in the cabaret scene in the movies. I wish I'd lived those times.

The age I live in, at this place, I was ill at ease. I felt I didn't belong here at all. I could never act like I was accustomed to this kind of demure place like some other people. There are some people who could pull it off very well, or they may really be from a good family. I felt myself started to hunch more and more. But tonight's dinner was in Rie's honor, I kept telling myself to pull together.

A couple of people said 'hi' to Stephen from the other table. Kira translated and described everything on the menu to Rie, and I joined in. I'd had so many questions regarding the menu but hesitated to ask to anyone. (I didn't know what 'seared skatefish with fennel sauce' was for instance. I imagined a fish with skates on its fins go round and round the Christmas tree at the Rockfeller Center. It must be a good friend with a dogfish . . .)

* * *

A man vs. three women, not to mention an American vs. three Japanese. Stephen was at a loss.

During the whole time, the conversation was carried (inevitably) in Japanese. Even when a topic started in English, it ended with a punch-line in Japanese. After three of us had a fit of laughter, there was no point to translate the joke. At one point Stephen said,

"You guys, talk! Don't worry about me."

Though I still felt obligated not to leave him out. After all he was our host, to honor his wife's friend's sister, not even a distant relative, and besides I knew the pain too well to sit with a bunch of people and not understanding what was going on. You'd feel yourself invisible.

I tried what I could, but my effort was getting nowhere. Partially because of Rie, in order to not alienate her we had to speak in Japanese, but moreover, what made it worse was Kira's reluctance to include Stephen. Somehow she seemed to have determined to shut Stephen out of the circle: every time I said something to Stephen, she'd interject in Japanese to steer the conversation her way. Subtly, she must have thought, but it didn't appear that way. Or she may not have cared one way or the other.

". . . And then, Rie, listen. . . .," and Rie would laugh.

Kira had Rie completely under her wing. Two of them were evidently having the great time, so I left it at that. (sorry, Stephen . . .)

"Stephen, my dear!"

When we were all working at desserts, a woman with enormous gold earings came up to him at the table.

"Hey!" Stephen got up immediately with a relief. Finally a rescuer.

They kissed, and the woman introduced him a guy she was with who stood discreetly behind her. A tall, dark and suave—his name was Albert. (Not English Albert with 't' sound, but Albert a la francais!) I feasted my eyes on him stealthily.

"Denise, Albert, this is Kira, my wife, and Rie and Satomi."

"Hello."

We exchanged smile. Only Albert stayed cool. From that I realized his job was only to please his elder companion. I wished I was in her position. It's not too bad getting old if you can have a guy like him in tow, I fancied.

Stephen and Denise chatted while Kira remained in her seat. At first she showed some courtesy, acting like an entrepreneur's wife should act, listening to their conversation without eagerly butting in, but after a while, when she noticed her presence wasn't required, she fished a cigarette out of her purse and lit it in silence. She inhaled smoke, kept it for a few seconds, and let it out with a long sigh. I expected her to look up and say something to change her mood, but she kept staring at the candle in the middle of table. She looked pale. I shot a glance at Rie in apprehension, and she too seemed to have sensed something was going wrong. We all fell in silent. Kira's mind was elsewhere. She didn't even notice my stare or anything else for that matter. I watched the tiny dots—the reflection of the candle in her eyes. For a while they stayed there steady as a bouy on the calm lake then suddenly flickered. Kira started fondling with the lacy cuff on her dress, squeezed it hard as she could, then, started to pulling it as if to tear the cuff apart like a mad woman who slashes her goose down pillows in frenzy, all while she kept her eyes at the candle. The chill ran down my spine. With the shiver, the noise of the room—that I wasn't even aware I'd lost—came back. I heard Stephen's laugh coming from above. Kira's shoulder shook, flames trembled in her eyes.

"Kira."

She came back to her senses and quickly wipe off a tear.

"Kira."

Hearing my voice, Stephen turned around. He glanced at me then at Kira.

"Anything the matter?"

A visible tension in his face.

"Nothing. Why?"

Kira pulled her best acting and feigned a smile.

". . . Well . . . ,"

Stephen looked at me suspiciously and said,

"It sounded like some commotion."

"No, really."

Kira said and smiled at Denise, who was looking at the two, taking an interest in what was going on.

Stephen gave Kira one last look and re-engaged in his conversation.

Kira's smile stayed there for a while as if she'd lost the control of it, then gradually, it slackened.

When she saw me looking at her, she took a beat to make up her mind, then let the words slip through between her teeth.

"Stephen's been seeing a girl."

23

There're so many things I just don't understand. And I'm confused. . . . .

The night Kira told me about Stephen, She never gave me a chance to say anything. There were no way we could talk about it, Stephen being there. Whether he understood Japanese or not. It's just the way it is, and Kira knew that, I'm sure. Then, why should she let it out then? I guess it just was the moment it happened to be. She probably just wanted to spill out. To unload the weight a little, perhaps. I don't even know for how long she kept it herself. Damn, if she had told me some another time and another situation, I could have talked over about it. I could have asked her questions—'how serious is it?' or 'how long has it been?', that type of 'fact-checking' questions. God, I sound like a nosey bitch, like I am burning with curiousty—as Rie had said. Maybe I am. No. . . . It's really hard to tell where curiosity ends and where friendly concern begins sometimes. But without knowing the 'facts' I can't assess the situation, therefore I can't advise—advise is not the word; I'm no better than she is, I don't know the world that well. Is there any other word?—Anyway if I knew a little more about it, I could think the matter with her. Or maybe she doesn't want that, knowing her being so proud. She must have kept it for a while to herself alone, and she may not have had the intention to tell anybody including me. It just so happened. She may be deep in a shame for telling me about it. It's very possible.

All these years of friendship, I've never heard any complaints or problems about their relationship, except time-to-time self-mockery. I always thought of her as pretty happy—lucky one. She had an apartment in SoHo, owned the half of the fabulous store, money in the bank, a well-off family and an American husband. A life I'd swap for in no time. . . .

But I guess life comes down on everybody once in a while.

Other thing I don't get is that they still live together, carrying on life as if nothing had happened. Even that very night Kira confided me about Stephen, they went home together nonetheless. I always—probably highly influenced by movies and comic books—thought when you are told by your husband or boyfriend that he is seeing somebody else beside you, you'd either dash out the house in a fury and desperation or disappear for a while till you find what to do. It may be a little silly and fanciful but particularly someone like Kira, who has a dramatic temperament and means of support, could have done anything she wanted, to go take a trip to Europe or wherever.

But she doesn't. Every night she goes home to the same place, shares the same bed with the traitor.

I don't know how she feels.

*   *   *

I want to call her. But how can I broach? She may be regretting, hating herself for telling me about it by now. . . .

Kira is a den mother—she never let her children see her tears. She is too proud—misfortune is not in her vocabulary.

I'd pick up the receiver, stare at the dialing buttons for a while then put it back. Over and over.

24

Not the Statue of Liberty, not the World Trade Center, not the Empire State—but there was one place Rie wanted to go—Coney Island.

"Coney Island? Why?"

I had to ask her. I'd been there long time ago. In a winter. The cold wind from the ocean was so strong it was almost like walking in a sand storm. The park was closed, so as all the places on the boardwalk. Only a hand full of stands facing the subway station stayed open, selling greasy hot dogs a few feet away from a real dog in rigor mortis.

"Oh, you must've been there at the wrong time. You gotta go there in a summer!" Rie exclaimed.

Then she told me about the movie she really loved—a movie that takes place in Coney Island.

"It's a love story between a guy who works in a burger joint and a girl—a mermaid. You see, the guy leaves his job after he has a fight with the big fat owner, goes to a showtent to kill some time, or let off the steam, whatever, sees this mermaid on a swing—and falls in love. Not knowing she's a real one. Then the problems start. . . ."

"Isn't that *Splash* ?"

I sneered. Talking about originality.

"Oh, no, doesn't *Splash* end happily? With Daryl Hannah getting legs from an incredible operation?"

"No, I don't remember."

"Me neither. Anyway, although they are in love, in the end they find they can't overcome the specific difference, so the guy takes her to the ocean and let her go back to her homeland—homesea, in this case? I don't know. . . .It's a fantasy, beautifully shot. The director, who also plays the guy is *sooo* talented."

She meant the actor she's been a big fan of for many years.

"You mean, this short order cook guy is a Japanese? It's not really convincing is it?"

"Oh, hc's supposed be a college drop-out. An American college, of course."

"I see. And the mermaid? Is she Japanese, too?"

I pictured some Japanese cutie *tarento* the dragging the tail of her oversized costume.

"No, she's an American. What's her name? She's pretty well-known . . . ah, I can't remember. . . .but it's really pretty movie, you'd like it. It's in black and white and the place looks so pretty. . . ."

"O.K,. O.K., we'll go."

I gave in.

The day we chose to go turned out be an overcast. The raging summer sun tried hard to break up the thick, chemical colored haze, but had no purpose. It wasn't picture-perfect kind of a day, though it may have been better off for us for not get sunburnt.

We took F train from Houston Street. The train came up overground just before the East River and went down again at the end of the bridge. It stayed down for a few stops then finally out in the daylight again till the last stop. I was enchanted by greenness of Brooklyn. You could see the trees and bushes; the various colored green patches everywhere, standing side by side with cozy looking houses.

As soon as we came out of the subway station, we were hit by the sweltering smell of heated oil. Dog stands were everywhere as far as you could see. They all had display of their main offering right above their sign in colored drawings. Not so tempting pictures of burgers, hot dogs, and french fries added the extra chaos to already deranged street.

We were struck by the number of people who were fooling around. It was only Thursday afternoon, but they were ready for the park and the beaches.

We first browsed to get the feel of the place, passing signs like, 'THE WORLD'S BIGGEST RAT' and 'INCREDIBLE TWO HEADED BABY', peeked at game stalls from behind the crowd.

"It's really working-class, isn't it? I love it!"

Rie said, watching an obviously immigrant family frolicking toward the beach.

"Yeah, I guess when you have enough money and a car, you'd go to Six Flags or something," I said.

As we got closer to the ocean, breeze began to freshen our sweaty bodies.

"Ooo—Nice!"

Rie lifted the hem of her t-shirt and fanned it.

"When you do that you look like a watermelon seller on a roadside," I teased.

"You're terrible!" Rie said in a mock-anger.

"Look, isn't that strange?"

Rie pointed at the abandoned roller-coaster. Under the impeccably rusted and rotten railings stood an equally old wooden house.

"Umm. . . ."

It looked certainly odd—the way the two stood together. The house was neatly tucked under the ride, like a relation of mushroom stem to its umbrella-part, the roof almost touching the base of the highest railings. There was no way you could tell which was built first, the ride or the house. Although you knew for sure one of them were meant to be removed for the sake of the other, you still couldn't figure out which was which. Oddly enough they seemed to have become one piece in a process of aging in oblivion. They looked like an eccentric old English couple which the wife henpecked the husband.

While we gazed out at them a couple in their thirties passed by and paused next to us.

"Do you remember in a Woody Allen movie, when he talks about growing up in a house under a rollercoaster?—That is it, you're looking at."

The guy pointed at it and told the girl.

"Hmm . . . Which Woody Allen movie?"
"Annie Hall."
After the two walked away, Rie was excited,
"It's a historic spot."
"I guess so." I shrugged.

*   *   *

We had a couple of intermediate rides—orange tickets in Disneyland; spinning teacup and pirate's ship. Then we advanced to the Cyclone, which I regretted as soon as the car started rolling down. It was a true terror: it didn't have any frills, no time to enjoy the height, it was built only to scare people to death relentlessly during its two minutes ride.

"I was this close from biting my tongue"

Rie said, making teeny space between her thumb and index finger, still shaking.

As we headed for the boardwalk, I looked up the railing of the ride we just came off and saw several brand new wood patches on the base of cross ties—I got scared twice more.

It wasn't so easy finding an empty bench along the boardwalk, but we managed to find one.

"Whoa, . . . finally," Rie collapsed on it, next to a Mexican youth in a thrash metal t-shirt. I could feel myself too was still wobbling from the ride.

"Awawawawawa. . . ." she mumbled and strecthed her neck.

The breeze was picking up its force, almost chilly. The

sun was nowhwere, perhaps hanging on really low behind the thick clouds. Many people were folding up the beach towels, shaking the sand off their bodies. Soon, in about a couple more hours the beach would be deserted, except for a few teenage couples. Watching a slow exodus of summer day made me feel nostalgic. I thought about the all the summers I've been through. A teenage summer day spent in a cave like cafe, a childhood summer in the sparkling water. . . .

"Do you remember when Father lost his glasses in the sea?" I asked Rie.

"Lost glasses . . . ? Oh, yeah, when we were visiting our grandma. He went into the water with his glasses on. . . ."

Rie laughed.

"Right. It was such a hubbub—We all walked up and down the beach to find them. Uncle Tadashi even swam around the shore with snorkeling goggles. The next few days till his new glasses were ready he had to live with his naked face. . . . It was so strange to see that—him without glasses."

"Yeah, I remember. Then as a child, I thought the reason Father wore glasses was to look formidable. In a way the look became him, wouldn't you say?"

"Do you mean you were scared of him too?"

I was startled with this new discovery.

". . . I always thought I was the one who got scolded and yelled at for no reason, and you're the one who was—I can't say 'loved', 'cause that's something I'm not sure he'd ever be capable of, but—fond of."

I spoke up the truth.

Rie thought about it a while she looked at the tip of her white sneakers and said,

"No, I wasn't scared. Just I was more cautious than you, not to set his bad temper on fire. . . . I learned a lot by watching you."

We became quiet. Right in front of our eyes, a Hispanic father with three children in a tow headed in direction of subway. His hands were full—with rolled up straw mats in one, supermarket plastic bags and towels in other, and with little hands of each child who tried to get hold of them. The mother followed smiling, holding another baby in her arm.

Rie and I both sighed at the same time.

We looked at each other in solemn expression, then,

"What was that?"

"You too."

We bursted into laughter.

We kept on laughing as long as we could while we worked on holding out weepy eyes from overflowing.

"Are you planning to have a baby?"

"Umm. . . . ."

Rie stretched her arms behind her ears then collapsed them around the head.

"Eventually. . . .yes. I want to have a baby."

She said decidedly.

" But it'll be a while till it happens. A long time."

She smiled but couldn't quite veil the bleakness.

"You want to get married first, right?"

I asked as I eyed on a lipstained cigarette butt caught between the wood panels of the boardwalk.

". . . .Sure. If it happens, it happens."

"You mean Masahiko doesn't say anything about it?"

"Yeah, he does. . . . He asked me to give him some time. After all his decision alone cannot change his life, you know?"

She was referring to his wife's reluctance to signing the divorce papers.

"I'm not sure myself if I care whether we get married or not, as long as he's single—divorced. It doesn't make a big difference to me. But if I was to have a baby, I want the baby to have a father. Not just his presence, but the legal status. . . . It may not matter here but in Japan a child born out of a wedlock will have a hard time. . . ."

With the toe of my shoes I tried to grub up the butt out of the crack.

". . . O.K., let's leave the baby out—but do you think you two may stay sort of fresh if you don't get married?

To keep the suspense, as people say?"

". . . Are you implying to Kira?"

Rie asked. I wasn't exactly thinking about it in her terms—But maybe I was.

"How did you . . . .?"

"Sorry, I didn't mean to, but I overheard it."

"Right. . . ."

I gave the butt a kick. It didn't go very far.

"Is it really serious?—it's a stupid question. . . . I know Kira looked completely shook."

"I don't know. I want to call her but——"

I confided Rie how I was unsure about going into business, that Kira may not want to me nosing in.

"You know when you get to a certain age the space

between you and your friends grows wider. You can't go into straight with a full-force at them anymore, not like the high school years where you had something in common with your friends: We were all the same age, single and lived with our parents. But at this point in life we all live in different circumstances, each surrounded by the world totaly unknown to the others. All of us got our own situations—We can't trespass others' domain with muddy feet and just say 'sorry!'."

Rie let the breeze sweep over her face then turned to me.

"Sis, you gotta call her—,"

She fixed her gaze on me and said,

"Don't even worry about whether she wants you to talk about the matter or not. I for sure know she wants it. . . . I think it's similar to what they call 'confessor's impulse'. . . . Once they admit their sin they just want to tell the priest the whole story. They want a priest to ask them questions, so they can put the things in perspective. . . . She has already thrown the key your way, it's your call to open it up. She really wants you to. You yourself know how it is, not to be able to find anywhere to set off. Even if she doesn't want to talk, she can't make a first move, can she? To say 'forget about what I said'? No. When you call her and if she doesn't bring it up, then you go along with her. No big deal, is it? Your call to her—that's all it takes."

"Ummm. . . . ."

"Can I be frank?"

I nodded.

"You tend to worry too much about what people think of you. You may be limiting yourself a lot by being that way."

"Do you think so?"

"Yeah, I do," she said.

25

(Do you want one too?)—Kira held out cigarettes in front of me without saying a word. I didn't know if I wanted it, but took one out anyway and lit it with a vermilion Bic that was lying on the floor. The first cigarette in many months tasted nauseating and made me dizzy. But I pulled another drag and watched the smoke diffuse then eventually dissolve into the air.

From her tone over the phone I knew she was really down but I somehow expected and hoped for her to greet me differently when I got here—No such luck. She opened the door in silence, except for a listless 'hi' and ushered me into the den, instead of the living room, where she seemed have been spending most of her time.

The room was dark for she'd had the theater like thick drapes closed, only the sharp rectangular of the sunlight edged in from between the cloths told what time of the day it was.

Kira sat on the floor in the middle of her empty birdcages, which varied in sizes and shapes. One of them was as big as you could possibly put an ostrich in, the rest were smaller, some made of thin matchstick like wood in Chinese style, others were in some kind of metal, somehow very German. Their semi-rusted bottom all had the indelible greenish white stains from their once upon a time occupants, and that gave this entire room the spooky air. It was as if all the birds just had flown away sensing a possible apocalypse.

Kira pulled on the cigarette, squinted quickly to avoid the smoke, exhaled it while gazed blankly at the ceiling. I kept my eyes on her every move, not so overtly for her to feel awkward but to catch any mood change so when she was ready I'd be right there to listen.

For a while—I didn't know exactly how long—five minutes? ten minutes?—we sat there on the floor. After a dry exchange on everyday topic, we seemed lost. She burried her face in her arms and stayed that way. From her motionless shoulders I knew she wasn't crying at least. I let her be.

Come to think of it I'd never been into this room, I was recalling. Except once, when I came over to this apartment for the first time she showed me around and presented her collection. She wasn't exactly thrilled to show me the whole place in detail, I'd thought, rather she was doing it because that what she was supposed to do—following the custom of this country.

"You know. . . .," a scratchy, frail voice came out of her. Every hair of my body perked up toward the voice. Her words stuck in a mid air for a brief second as if they were pinned, then she cleared her throat.

". . . . Just before I entered grade school, my family moved to a countryside from the city. . . . It wasn't your postcard image of a country—sure, there were fields and chicken farms and stuff, but it was more like a commuter's town in progress. Local farmers' families and newly arrived commuter families, in, I say, a seventy to thirty ratio. . . ."

She cleared up her throat again in a little embarassment and said,

". . . .I really don't know where to start but I'm trying my best . . . It may be a long way around but so many things go round and round my head these days, so bear with me . . . ?"

I nodded reassuringly.

". . . Kids there more or less played outdoors; even girls would ride around on bikes, play war games just like boys and I couldn't believe it. For all I know, my friends from the city always wanted play indoors, with dolls and crayons. They weren't interested in getting themselves dirty with soil, and neither was I. . . . I don't think I was being a city snob, it was a matter of personal preference, you know?"

I gave her a nod.

"But kids thought I was so stuck up. They thought I was a princess who lived in a castle, and didn't want to mingle with underclass. You know how kids are—they're always looking for someone to pick on—and they chose me. They started calling me names—'mutt', 'mongrel', 'mixed scum', etc. etc. . . . These words don't rub me or anything now, just like being called 'bimbo'. . . . But then, as a kid those words would kill you, especially when you didn't have anybody by your side. Basically they picked on the way I looked. Then I had carrot-orange hair and a bunch of freckles, actually looked lots more outlandish than I do now. The curious thing was, it was around the time you saw so many half-breeds on television and magazines, being treated like they were jewels. But somehow the idea never took hold of its root in the country-suburb I lived in. It's probably because the town was situated right next to the U.S. Air base, and being a half-breed meant a bastard. That was the take of the adults anyway, so consequently that idea was handed down to kids. . . . . It's so unimaginable from these days, isn't it? When everyone wants to internationalize themselves?

"First it was calling me funny, and then after they noticed that I didn't show any reaction, they took another step: They stoned me. Once. I guess they just wanted to see me cry and didn't mean a big harm. . . . But nonetheless a stone hit me in the belly, I tried not to cry, because I knew that was all they wanted and I wasn't gonna give them the satisfaction. So I bit my lips hard, held my belly and dragged myself home. Thinking, 'why me? I'm not even a real mixed blood. Why? Why? Why?'

As the pain became acute so did my anger. I remember thinking, as deranged as I was, 'O.K. . If you can't accept me, I won't accept you. I'm going someplace else where I can be with people who look like me, who don't pick on me. You watch.'. . . ."

Kira grinned in self-mockery, and pulled her hair behind her back. I waited her to continue.

"Sure, everybody grows out of their child trauma and so did I. I made some friends and lived there like everybody else. In other words I didn't make my conscious decision to come live in the States based on the childhood grudge. . . . . But still, when things get tough, a part of me starts to think, 'What in the hell am I doing here? Am I here not because I like it here but because I can't stand living in Japan?'. . . ."

Kira looked away and clammed up. I thought of my sister's saying about confession (where did she get that from anyway?)—she was probably right about that. I began to realize there was a lot more than just Stephen's having an affair. Kira seemed to ge groping in the darkness of her world to find a core.

"Do you remember the store we used to have on La Guardia Place?"

For a moment I didn't get who 'we' were. Then I shook my head sideways.

"Ah, so it was before I met you. Before we moved to Greene Street, we had a store on La Guardia Place. It was such a teeeny little place—if you put a couch, it'd fill up the whole space—that kind of place. It was nice, I don't mean the place, but our state of mind. . . .We had something definite to dream about—to have a store in SoHo someday. You see, where we were was close enough, but we weren't in there. It was only one block away, but we weren't in SoHo. Even our street changed its name when you crossed Houston.

Everyday we'd stand in front of the store and look southward—to the other side of Houston—and picture it. Dreaming together like that meant a lot to us, made us feel like a unit. As young as we were, and as scared as we were, we had the spirits to protect each other from any terrible disaster. . . ."

Kira stopped and sniffed.

"God, I can't believe it was only a few years ago. And now this!"

She said it loud, perhaps just let it out, to no one in particular.

"Kira—"

I stretched my arm to hold her quivering shoulder. She picked up a tissue and wiped her nose.

". . . .Sorry. I'm pathetic, aren't I?"

She drew a deep breath to hold any more tears from coming out.

"No, don't be silly. . . ."

I said hastily. Maybe she should break down and cry that may be the best thing—I felt utterly useless.

". . . .You know, when he told me he'd been seeing somebody for more than a few months, I was in awe at first. 'It can't be!'—then soon afterwards I realized I'd somehow expected something like that to happen. It wasn't like I was looking forward to it, but I felt I'd waited, even manipulated myself so that things would turn out that way . . . Oh, it'd have happened anyway. I may be saying that to save my ego. . . . I don't know.

For a while now I've been feeling I was left behind. By everything. The store has become virtually his. The business has grown, but so have the other things that go with it, accounting matters especially. Stephen has always been good at this but I wasn't. When our business became from plain retail to import-export, I just couldn't keep it up. New words, new terms everyday. I always thought my English was O.K., but I found it wasn't good enough to operate the business. So the responsiblites shifted more and more to Stephen. And gradually I started feeling left out. From the store, from everything. That was about when I began to resent him. I just couldn't accept that everything was running smoothly without having me around. I wasn't needed.

I thought about starting something on my own, something small, manageable. But I didn't know exactly what I wanted right away, and since Stephen didn't mind me keeping my position as a paper-partner, I rode on. I kept thinking, I'm gonna do something, I'm gonna do it, then all of a sudden found myself too scared to do anything. If I was five, no, even three years younger I could have thought about restarting my life, maybe, making drastic changes. But I can't now. . . . I wasn't like this before as far as I remember. I used to be more out going, independent, especially when I lived in Japan. I can't help thinking that. What happened to me? Here, with English, I'm only a second class citizen forever. With my accent, lack of vocabulary, not a full person. . . . Then I'd think Japan could be easier in a lot of ways but I don't think I can adjust back so well with my age. I'm too used to being here—everything is a little more personable. I belong neither here nor there, you know? . . . I sometimes cannot help thinking that it may be easier for me if something terrible happened to Stephen—if he was gone from this world, then I can start living my life again. I'd be forced to, so I would have no choice but to carry on all by myself. . . . I know it's a horrible thought. . . .

"You know, I just can't stop picturing the woman—A girl, twenty-six, Sorbonne graduate American who lives in Rome——Is she pretty? Has she got a beautiful Western body? Smile? How does she love him? Do they kiss each other in a park? In a theater? Cafe? Does she please him a lot? The thoughts just tear me apart. . . . . He may be with her right now, as we talk. It's just. . . . For Stephen hasn't taken any interest in whatsoever I do for a long time now. And perhaps I in return am doing the same to him. . . . . ."

Kira squeezed her eyelid. Hard. She looked like a war prisoner about to be shot.

I drew a deep breath and asked her.

"Do you still love Stephen?"

Her whole body froze. For a moment, she showed a face of a little girl lost.

". . . .I think so as far as I know. . . .Then again, I may be trying to convince myself to think that way for fear of getting separated, having to go my own way. . . . ."

She drew up her knees under the chin, rested her face on the upperarm. The expression of her face was obscured by it.

". . . What does Stephen say? Do you know what he wants?"

As soon as the words came out my mouth, I wondered I was getting into too deep.

She shook her head wearily.

"He doesn't even know it himself—that's what he says. He doesn't know *yet.*"

I wondered how come Stephen couldn't have kept his mouth shut. He didn't have to tell Kira about the girl, did he? Whether it was out of guilt or courtesy, he shouldn't have told her, if just to confuse her. . . .

"Maybe you want to take a trip somewhere for a while for a change of the mood. Have you thought about that?"

"Me? Travel where? I'll be. . . , no. I can't. I don't feel like doing anything. I can't go anywhere, I don't want to. I can't go to Japan—"

"Why?"

I felt ridiculous asking her that.

"Because, once I go back there, our personal matter would become a family matter, whether I like it or not."

—'You can't go back because of your vanity', I said to myself. Then I felt sorry for both of us. Why do we always have to compare our life in a new country to a war? Do we *have to* feel defeated by the country? Why can't we simply say our temperament didn't agree with the place . . . ?

I didn't know how long we stayed in the den surrounded by the cages. Silence brooded over us with a haze of smoke. Even an air-conditioner didn't seem to clear all it out. I went to the window and saw the Empire State gleaming in the orange sun, its wall surface looked as placid as a mirror. I looked at my watch; it was time for work.

I paused a little so as to decide what to do. Shall I leave now or shall I stay? Although still pensive, Kira seemed to be stable enough to be left alone.

"Kira. . . . ."

"I know you gotta go."

She said with acute awareness which took me by surprise.

"Well, yeah——"

I mumbled, feeling awkward having been read my mind.

"But if you want me to, I—"

"Oh, don't worry—", she interjected.

"I'll be fine."

She fluttered her hand like a butterfly as if to chase bad spirits away. She even had a slight smile on her face.

"Are you sure?"

I looked into her eyes in demand of a straight answer.

"Yeah, is there anything wrong with me?"

She opened her arms and made a little grin.

"Oh, Kira."

I felt it was too early to respond her with smile. She may well be pulling the bravado.

"Satomi, c'mon——"

She stood up and stretched her arm to take my hand.

"Here, I'll show you the door."

She led me through the living room.

"Are you really sure, now?"I pressed.

"Of course . . . You know, it didn't happen yesterday. I'll live through it ."

She made a vague smile in resignation. Mac came and rubbed his head against Kira's feet.

I couldn't find what to say so I nodded.

". . . Don't do anything stupid, all right?"

I had to say this. I tried to deliver as lightly as I could while I kept my eyes on Mac.

"Stupid. . . .? Oh, no, Don't have to worry about that. I have enough reasons to stick around. . . .for my new clothes for instance."

Kira broke into a half smile.

When the elevator door was about to close Kira called, "Satomi."

"Yes?"

I looked for a 'open door' button but wasn't quick enough.

"Thanks."

The elevator door closed before I had a chance to say anything.

26

There are days I can't get out of bed. When I open my eyes and see a leaden sky smeared with factory wastes, I want to quit everything, cover myself with the sheet again and go back to sleep. Until my next life.

27

"Kira is late, isn't she?" Rie said, getting slightly apprehensive.

I looked at my watch again. Quarter to twelve. I stood on tiptoe, looked both side of the street in hopes to find her bouncy walk. Still no sign of Kira. I glanced at the bouncer who stood sternly in front of the doorway emotionless.

We were suppose to meet up here at eleven-thirty. It was Kira's idea to take Rie out before she left New York.

"Oh, you know she never comes on time. Never."

I'd meant to assure her of usualness of Kira's not showing up on time, but then I questioned whether I'd given just the opposite effect.

We stood there while various types of people—club kids in a baggy clothes, Wall Street type couple, Latinos from the neighborhood—all went inside. After a few antsy checking up with my watch, when it said almost midnight I decided to give her a call. I hoped she hadn't forgotton our date. It couldn't be.

I left nervous Rie to stand closer to the bouncer, just in case Kira got there while I was on a phone.

I rang, for ten rings—no answer, not even an answering

machine. I tried again, in case I misdialed. 4XX-2XXX. . . . Same thing. No answer. I hung up wondering where she was. Is she on her way here? Or. . . .? I went back to the enterance area brusquely.

"She's not there?" Rie asked.

"No." I said as I looked around to see if an occupied cab was approaching.

When she suggested we three go out for one last time, she was definitely in up mood. Knowing her, one assumed there could have been a little acting involved, but I was pretty sure she really was more optimistic that day than she had been in a while. She talked about possibility of taking some courses in interior design, which I thought was good idea since she seemed have a flair for it. Furthermore it would do her good to occupy her time with something like that, and I told her so.

"Exactly," she said gaily.

"I can't be moping forever, can't I? It's my life and if I don't get a grip on it, who will, right?"

But where is she? Is she. . . .?

———No, I'm too much of a worrywart—I kept telling myself to hold back the growing anxiety.

Then a cab came around Essex Street. Could it be?—Rie and I fastened our eyes in desperate hope. Soon the door opened and there came out a girl in a coat. A coat in this weather? But it was her.

"Kira!"

Rie and I called out in unison.

"I'm really sorry I'm late. . . .," she apologized kind of offhandedly.

I was rather benumbed but kept my composure. She got here after all.

"Let's go in."

she motioned us with an enchanted smile.

"What happened to you?" I called out to Kira, but once we were inside I had to give up asking. Heavy salsa music was blaring everywhere in the electric-blue room to carve our body in curvy figure. It looked pretty busy for the midweek night. (Although I didn't have any measure to compare it to—since I'd not been in a club in a longest while.)

We got some drinks from the bar and sat ourselves in a nearby table. A group of guys glided their eyes on us nonchalantly but piercingly. I fell into the well of self-consciousness right away. This kind of immediate examination of one's desirabilty was something I'd forgotten for a long time.

Unable to return my gaze to see if anybody was still watching, I turned to the dance floor. Several couples were getting it on pretty passionately in the middle of the crowd. Salsa and latin temperament—you can't beat them when it comes to openness of sexuality. I took a sip of my vodka tonic to cheer me on.

The right of me, Kira and Rie drew close chatting and laughing boisterously. A couple of Latin American looking guys (Colombian?) beamed at us. Kira pretended she didn't take notice, I could tell, from the way she ignored them completely.

To me Kira's laugh didn't seem so genuine. It was too exaggerated and forced, but nonetheless it made me let out the sigh of relief. I'd much rather see her up and spiky than gloomy and pitiable.

"Let's ask Satomi," Kira turned her glowing face to me.

"What's that?"

"Rie and I are in the middle of ranking the most desirable man in this place. We are about to pick the semi-finalists—which do you think, that guy (she pointed discreetly with her forefinger) in the v-neck or that rasta?"

I examined both of them.

"Umm. . . . . ."

I'd normally go for the rasta but with this one I wasn't sure. He was too—I didn't even know. He was just—off. Maybe it was his muscles. On the other hand, you never see any skinny rastas. Maybe you gotta go to Jamaica for them.

"I don't know,"I said.

"You don't know? C'mon, what a bore!"

I guess I am, I thought.

"Yeah, C'mon, Sis!"

Rie joined the force. It seemed both of them had finished the drink. Already.

"But look, first of all what's the point of comparing two guys in similar physical types? They are too macho, both of them. Secondly, the guy in the hideous v-neck has gotta be gay."

"So?" Kira contested,

"If you stick to the reality, how many of do-ables are there in this room—two?"

I laughed and shrugged.

* * *

"Two vodka-cranberry," Kira had to screamed at waitress' ear.

While I finished a glass, Rie and Kira downed three.

"Are you sure?"

I looked at both of them.

"Why not?" Kira said jovially, in a meantime Rie nodded happily next to her.

The place looked like on its peak. It wasn't full but well crowded with people who you couldn't tell what they did for living.

For some time now, I'd been feeling the intense gaze coming from the certain spot of the room. One of the Colombians who sat with a couple seemed to take interest in us. I turned my head slowly to see if he was still there. He was. Our eyes met, he made a grin from under his mustache without moderating the gaze. I immediately looked away to Kira.

I saw Kira smiling back at him. She sat erect, crossed her legs with a great care, as if she was ready for the challenge. She was about take up one of her favorite roles of cool but irresistable, femme fatale.

It didn't take too long for the Colombian to come over to our table.

"May I join you for a moment?" he asked with very little trace of an accent, to my surprise.

"If you like," Kira said hospitably.

"Thank you," he saluted and pulled a chair.

Up close he looked a lot younger, it was his prematurely receded hairline that gave him a look of well middle aged man.

"Where are you ladies from?"

Kira gave a quick glance at Rie and me and said,

"Hong Kong."

Then burst out laughing.

The guy seemed staggered, a little ticked, but regained the composure soon enough.

"Oh, C'mon now. Let me guess—"
"Japan——Isn't that obvious?"
Kira said with a irreverent smile.
"Not necessarily . . . Are you visiting?"
"Visiting whom?"
"The city. New York. Aren't you tourists?"
"No. I live here."
Kira declared, not being hasitant to show a little annoyance. I nodded at her side.
"Oh."
He reacted rather being let down.
"How about you? Aren't *you* a tourist?"
Kira asked somewhat thorny.
"No, I've been here for five years."
"Oh, yeah? I've been seven."
"Really?"
He looked hard at Kira perplexed, probably puzzled about her possible age.
"What do you d——?"
"Where are you from?"
Kira cut out the guy's question, instinctively knowing that could lead to her means of living—marital status.
"I'm from Chile."
"Oh, really?"
Kira responded in a rather exaggerated manner.
"Yes. Why? Do you have any Chilean friends?"
"No, I thought you were Colombian—and I was so sure you had a little packet of powder in your pocket."
The guy frowned.
"Oh, I'm sorry. It was in a bad taste."
Kira smiled and reached for his hairy hand.

"Forgive me."

She covered his hand softly with her two hands.

The guy made a pout then nodded.

"Thank you," she said meekly, then fished out a cigarette.

"Allow me," he held back her hand and grabbed the lighter and lit the cigarette.

"Gracias."

"De nada."

The guy said, and began stroking Kira's hand.

I looked at Rie in embarrasment: she was also blushing.

"Shall we?"

Kira asked the Chilean, holding out her arms across the table.

He bowed courteously and escorted her down to the dance floor.

There the two danced, retaining a certain distance as if to study the goods they each were about to purchase.

Kira, who had a cigarette between her fingers swayed her hips like a teenage whore who was scheming up something to trick the guy. She teased him with a sultry twist of her body, loosely parted lips, toss of her hair, as the guy glided his eyes like a tongue.

I was getting uneasy. Watching her do overtly sexual moves was gradually driving me into the desperation. I wanted get out and scream. That body of hers. . . . .

". . . .Do you think it's all right?"

Finally Rie said, as she watched the progress.

After the music changed to a slow ballad, Kira and the Chilean buried their faces, almost gobbling at each other's throat. Their legs were joined at their pelvis, her diamond earrings gristened each time she threw her head back.

It was mere surprise they hadn't gone down on the floor yet.

I felt my body began to heat up from the spectacle, and from the dull aggrevation that was building up steadily inside. Aggravation for what? I didn't know myself.

"Shall we go soon?. . . I wanna go before I get too depressed," Rie said. She looked a little ill.

"*Sh*. . . .," I tapped her hand.

"Let's see what happens," I said.

After a few more songs Kira came back to our table, grinning wildly with her smudged lips. I bit mine.

"*Phew*.. . . . ."

She drew out a long breath in content, smoothes up her dress and reached for her purse.

"We wanna go soon," I said flatly.

Kira took her compact out, checked her face quickly and put it back in the purse.

"Kira."

She at last looked at me and winked.

"Buona notte."

She breathed out alcohol smell into my face.

"Kira?"

She grabbed her coat off the chair and scurried out the room with the Chilean.

28

I went down the dark staircase that led to the grotto. Ahead of me were a few village people dressed in colorful sarongs. The cave was massive: the light from the candles that were lit to bless the statue of Buddha threw the vague golden rings against its rugged walls. We were here to collect bat's dung to be used as the fertilizer for the village farms. We squated down and started working. We used a wood ladle to scoop. Now and then I heard a small thing, perhaps as light as a tiny bird nest, fell off from above and landed with a soft thump down below.

"What's that?"I asked.

"Don't look."they said.

Then I realized they were the small bat babies falling from the mother's body.

"Those silver worms will suck at anything."

I nodded and kept on working. When the tip of my ladle hit something a little crusty, I picked it up and brought to my eye level. It was whitewashed skelton of a bat with an agonized face——

Then a phone rang. . . . . . .

* * *

. . . . The phone rang. I jumped up from my bed and looked at the clock. 7:08 am. Who's calling this early? Something happened to Kira?—My heart began to race up.

Rie was awake and looked at me. From the look in her face—besides looking a little hung over—I could tell we were thinking the same thing, but neither of us spoke. The phone kept making the sinister noise. It didn't seem to give up. I gulped down the saliva at the fifth ring and picked it up.

Click.

". . . Hello."

Only the willowy, scratchy voice came out my throat.

"Hello, *moshi-moshi*? Is this *Ms.* Rie's sister? Did I wake you up?"

The relief and annoyance rushed against each other in my gut.

". . . .No. Don't worry. . . ."

"Ah. . . . ."

Neither he seemed to know what to say.

". . . . How are you?"

"Fine, thank you. . . . Here's Rie."

I handed Rie the phone. She had a million dollar smile on her face.

"Moshi-moshi, Masahiko——"

I stood up and went to the sink. I opened the faucet as far as I could and splashed the cold water on my face. Though we'd left the fan on all night, my forehead felt sticky. I looked myself in the mirror and quickly looked away. I went into the toilet and sat there for a while—until Rie finished her phone call.

"Whatever happened to him?"

I said to Rie as I sat down on the bed.

"Sorry. He just wanted to make sure he'd catch me. Basically he wants me to get a Chivas Regal in a duty-free. Provided he comes to the airport to carry it home."

She giggled. Her whole face was glowing.

"Hmm . . . Nice. . . . . But you know what? He addressed me as "*Ms.* Rie's sister'——it sure feels really strange. I have my name, and besides, even I'm your big sister, I'm still a lot younger than him, ain't I?"

"Umm. . . .Well, maybe he's not sure what is polite since you guys never actually met . . . you know?"

"Maybe."

I shrugged.

* * *

That whole morning I thought about Kira. Did she get home all right? Or is she even home? Is she safe? Is she. . . . All the worries popped my mind now and then and every time I had to tell myself to calm down——that everything was O.K. .

I wanted call her to see how she was, but I was worried to wake her up. If she was asleep, I wanted let her sleep. So I made up my mind to call her in the evening, after five. Even if she'd been asleep all day she'd be up by then, I figured.

Noon came, three o'clock came, then five——.

I didn't want to call her at the dot of five as if I'd set the alarm for it——But when my clock said 5:03, I couldn't wait any longer. Ten hours of waiting was long enough. I dialed the number.

Twl. . . . . Twl. . . . . Twl. . . . . .

"Hello."

———!

It wasn't Kira.

". . . .Hello? Is this 4XX-2XXX?"

"Yes, it is."

! Who is this person? WHAT'S GOING ON?——I didn't know what to think. Could this be, could this be Stephen's girlfriend?

I felt my blood draining .

"Who is this? Is Kira there? Stephen?"

I must've sounded like a estranged lover threatening the former girlfriend at a gun point in a TV drama.

"My name is Janet, and I work for Stephen. . . .Are you Kira's friend?"

"Yes."

There was a brief silence.

"Hello?"

"Um . . . I'm not sure if I have the right to tell you this, but Kira's in a hospital."

"NO!"

For a moment I saw nothing.

29

I ran and ran. Like I never did, and never will for probably the rest of my life.

First I dashed out to the First Avenue to catch a cab. I stood there at the corner of First and Twelfth, but there was no free cabs, none whatsoever. It couldn't be helped. It was raining too damn hard. Why today? Why now? I ran up to the Fourteenth whlle looking back at times to see if I'd spot one. I was hoping to catch a crosstown cabbie, but no luck. If I kept standing at one spot I may have been lucky, but there was no way I could stand tight with my state of mind. I had to be moving. I had to be getting closer, closer to Kira.

I ran like a maniac, and nearly threw people off the street a couple of times. I almost tripped with a leash and choked the little Yorkshire.

"Watch it!" the old woman in a vinyl babushka yelled and I screamed back at her,

"Don't walk your dog in the rain!"

With the umbrella in my hand it was tough to run, but I kept on. Until I finally snatched one just in front of NYU medical.

Once settled in I wiped my rain soaked hair with my coat. To my fortune, the cab driver didn't pay any attention to me. I mean in a situation like this I could't have made any conversation. I took deep breath a few times to try to steady myself, but it wasn't so easy.

As the cab sped toward uptown, I couldn't help feeling that I'd been into the same situation before. A deja vu, I guess it was. Though it wasn't possible. Then I began to wonder if somewhere back of my mind I'd been rehearsing this moment——that Kira was in hospital and I was rushing over there. I really didn't know.

When I came to the door I was directed to(I had to tell them I was her sister), I took a deep breath. My quickened pulse had died down, but I was still breathing short and shallow. But then once I was there and I couldn't delay any moment, so I knocked gingerly and opened the door.

The first thing I saw in the bare little room was Stephen. He sat there next to the modular bed, his hair all messy, leaning forward.

"......."

Stephen turned. I looked at his pale face that accentuated his freckles a lot more than usual. We looked each other in silence; neither of us had *a* word to say. My tongue was throbbing like I just had burned it. The anticipated anger I'd thought I might have wasn't there when I actually saw him.

I tightened my mouth. Stephen made a slight nod and

by the incline of his head he beckoned me. I saw he had Kira's hand in his as if he was clinging to it.

"Kira. . . . ."

As I barely called her name under the breath, tears welled up my eyes. It was she but it wasn't. She looked as if all her life was drained out of her. So gaunt. It was more credible to be told she'd gone than she was alive.

She opened her eyes half way, recognized me and quickly looked away. It pained me. Maybe I shouldn't have come. But I couldn't leave the room either. I hung my head down.

The room was filled with silence except the sound of gusty rain splashed against the window. I noticed a well-worn suitbag and a suitcase with various tags sat in one corner. Stephen must have flown in from somewhere. He still had his coat on.

Kira kept her face turned away, eyes closed. As if by doing so she could become invisible—from me, from Stephen, and perhaps from herself.

Stephen tapped my shoulder. I looked at him in plead. He looked down away from me. I nodded helplessly, and let him escorted me towards the door.

"*Matte.*"

Kira said in Japanese. I turned around.

"Could I have a few minutes with Satomi?"

She asked Stephen.

"Honey, but. . . . ."

"For a few minutes. . . ."

". . . . . Sure."

He paused for moment then nodded.

". . . I'm going to the cafeteria. . . . Do you want anything?"

"No. Thank you."

"Satomi?"

"Thank you, no."

I shook my head.

". . . . . O.K. ."

Stephen nodded twice, clasped his hands tightly around hers and left the room.

I sighed. At last the room became ours. Kira snd I alone.

I pulled up a chair and got closer.

She looked at me blankly, and I didn't know whether I should smile. Or cry. Or. . . . . .

As though reading my mind, Kira averted her eyes. The air between us was dense and damp, as if we were two broken pieces from a shipwreck floating in the ocean, away and away from each other. It was somehow fatal.

"So . . . how do you feel?"

Silly as it may sound, I couldn't think anything else. I felt a nausea in my stomach.

". . . . . . Tired."

She said wanly, with her face turned away.

I nodded.

". . . . I'm sorry, maybe I shouldn't have dashed to come see you. . . . But when I called you this girl answered the phone and. . . . ."

"A girl? Who?"

She turned her face.

"I believe her name was Janet."

"Oh, Janet. . . ."

She sighed. I waited but she kept staring at the ceiling.

What exactly happened to you?—was a question swept around my head. Janet only told me Kira was rushed to the hospital but was O.K. . I wasn't sure if she was hiding something from me, or that was really all she knew, but either way she wasn't going to say any more than that.

"It was just an accident. I didn't mean to kill myself."

Kill myself——those words rang heavy in my head.

"It's true. I felt shitty and wanted to sleep to forget it. That's all really."

I could see she was a little agitated although she must be under some kind of sedation. Maybe it was not a good idea to let her talk——but I couldn't resist to find out. Somehow I felt if I didn't hear from her now I'd never hear the truth of the matter.

I heard someone racing in the hallway. The peculiar sound of nurse's sneakers passed, then a few pairs followed. I felt ill at ease as if they were rushing into the room in any minute. Kira blankly stared at the ceiling.

After the hallway became quiet again, she murmured.

". . . . . . I almost killed the cat."

"The cat? What cat?"

I wasn't sure what she was talking about.

"Mac."

30

Now I know nobody is going to believe me that I didn't try to finish myself off. I really didn't. I swear. Unless I had made some kind of unconscious decision before that without me—the conscious me—realizing. Who knows. That I have to leave to Satomi, that's her territory. That night when I came home I was at my absolute bottom. I was supposed to feel better after I slept—I mean made it—with the Chilean. He said his name was Peter—Pedro, but I didn't believe him. For he took me to some apartment to screw me, I saw him take out one set of keys first and quickly put them away and take out another set. That place must have belonged to his friend or something, otherwise why did he have two separate sets? Anyway we went inside to this truly non-descript apartment furnished with obvious D. I. Y. furniture. Like a college dorm. I hated them. We sat on this unvarnished couch with a miserable purple and green patterned cushions. He came on to me then and there which I wasn't so thrilled about, so we moved to yet unvarnished bed. He wasn't so bad, as far as a one night stand goes, you know. I could have been carried away, I was drunk enough, and if this guy could have given me some kind of pleasure which I hadn't experienced in a while, I should have gone with it. But I couldn't. All this time I was with him I was so aware that I was only doing it to compete with Stephen. I wasn't there to get fucked for a fucking purpose, I wasn't there because I was lonely for some flesh, I wanted to fuck him only to tell Stephen later—How would he react? Would he get hurt? Serves him right! He should know how it feels—then on the other hand he might not care at all. Not even a twitch in the eye—

When I started thinking that I felt too lousy. Deplorable, disgusted and yet pitiful.

I came home but shittiness stayed the same. And all of a sudden I couldn't take it anymore. What am I doing? Why am I here? If I put an end to myself today, is the world gonna mourn me? Miss me? No! The truth is nobody cares. I exist in my world, but even when I'm gone from the world, it'll still exist without me, without hindrance to anybody, anything. The thought was already killing me . . .

At that point I was ready to go. Ready to get it over with. It didn't seem too hard at all. I mean I can never throw myself from a building nor pop a gun into my head, I'm not that courageous, but swallowing pills seemed nothing to me. Nothing unusual. Just an extention of daily life, just this time there'll be no waking up. The one way ticket to eternity. Good-bye, adieu, arrivederci! Only thing I was reluctant to leave was my cat. But he'll be taken care of—Stephen liked him, too. He can carry on his life just the same. Then somehow I started to picture Stephen living happily with his girlfriend and *my* cat! My cat living with them! *That* I couldn't take it. Mac was mine. Not ours, but mine. I had to leave it as is. Nobody's gonna change, nobody's gonna claim him. . . .so. . . .

I started to fill the bathtub with the water—I couldn't find any other way. I sat on the toilet, waited till the tub was full enough to cover the height of the cat, then I grabbed Mac and stood next to the tub. He didn't resist for he was always fascinated by the water. Everytime I filled the tub, he'd be right there gaping at it, with his front paws on the edge of the tub, standing tiptoe. . . . I watched the waterline rise. I was mesmelized by it. The faucet, the water, the force. The water looked gushing out from the drain, rather than coming out of the faucet. I held him tight, as hard as I could. Despite all that much fur, he was so tiny under my grip. His fat was soft like a rabbit's. I started wondering why he weren't my child. He was my baby, but he wasn't growing up. . . . He'd never be able to take care of himself. If he could I wouldn't need to do this. . . . I desperately wished he could. . . . Then he scratched me and got away. Perhaps the animal instinct—he got up the top of the refridgerator where I couldn't reach. I tried to get hold of him, but he drew back. He looked at me in complete mistrust. My heart shrieked.

There was nothing I could do. I couldn't do *it*. I sat on the floor for a while until I came up with other solution. . . . .

I took a cab to Washington Square. It was just before the daybreak and maybe because it was summer there were plenty of people around. I was kind of relieved. You know it's funny that a person who is willing to take in her life still worries about being mugged. I guess we're scared of the nature of unexpected events, especially when it comes to violence. . . .

I got to eastern side of the square where there were big trees, and opened the cat's box. He didn't want to come out of it first, I had to coax him. Once he was out, I could see he was shocked. He looked around him with jerky moves of his head, absolutely stunned. Can you imagine he never had been out of the apartment, and all of a sudden, this! He stayed there on the same spot and looked at me. I thought it was a look of plead at first, like he was asking me not let him go. But after all he's a cat, no matter how sedated life he had, he was still an animal. He saw something moved in the grass and there he went. By and by further and further from me. I was kind of happy that I did something good for him before I went, and for me too, finally seeing him act like the way he should act—after all cats are related to bigger cats in the wild, aren't they? I almost broke down with tears. Then all of a sudden fear sneaked in to me—What if he was picked up by some wacko? Who would just enjoy tormenting animals?——I have seen a little mutt covered with hundreds of burns. The owner told me some mental had branded the dog with cigarette butts.

I didn't want Mac to fall into hands of someone like that. I didn't want him to suffer, never, never—Only a few minutes ago this same person—I was gonna finish him off with her own hands!

I panicked and started to look for him all over. God, I must've been crazy to let Mac go like that! I called out for him, as I got threatened by the people who were still sleeping there. By this time I came back to my senses I guess, realized I'd been completely insane, out of my mind. I wanted the cat back. I called and called all around the park, and you know that park is not small. I got exhausted. The alcohol was still holding court in my stomach. I didn't know for how long I'd been looking for him till this punk kid came up to me and told me if I was looking for a cat, he'd seen it near the staue. So I dashed, searched around there all over. Then finally I heard a feeble meow . . . I whistled to get him respond. "Mac, Mac."

Then I finally saw him up on a small tree! I had no idea he could climb up a tree! But there he was perched on a branch, lost and scared, perhaps he'd gone up there to avoid dogs. . . . He didn't want to come down so I jumped up a few times with my heels to shake him off the tree.

I got him home. On the way I was feeling how silly the whole thing was. It was worse than a comedy show on television. I didn't want to remember the whole thing I just wanted forget, go to sleep. Next morning I'd be crisp, I thought. But when I opened the door to my place the water was everywhere. It was like the roof had blown away in the middle of a hurricane. Apparently I'd forgotton to turn off the bathtub. I almost lost my mind. I couldn't think anything else to do, so I took my pills to just knock myself out. I couldn't deal with it then. . . .

The next thing I knew was I was being pumped up my stomach.

I was told the super had found me, he had the complaint from the tenant down below. It must have leaked pretty bad. . . . It was a lake in our place. . . . ."

*　　*　　*

Neither of us spoke for a longest while. Kira drew a deep breath and closed her eyes. I watched the sharp needle of the rain illuminated by the light from the room. We sat there like some old sisters who had spend their whole life together, appreciated each other's company but nothing whatsoever to say to each other.

Another restless night was edging in.

"I'm going to Minnesota."

Kira said.

"Believe it or not, to a detox. It's really exaggerated, but it's the best thing for me and for Stephen. . . . . I can have time of my own there. . . . ."

"For how long?"

"A month or so."

A month! It seemed eternal.

"What are you going to do there? You know you'll be bored."

I said out of spite.

Kira made a faint smile while she kept her eyes closed.

When I came out of the hallway, I saw Stephen sitting in a waiting area. He was making fists and then opening them. Then fists, then open, perhaps he wasn't aware of what he was doing. He was staring at an old poster of MOMA exhibit of Impressionists. When he took notice of me standing next to him, he stopped his gripping exercise.

We hugged each other in silence. Tenderly and yearningly, as if it was a reunion of lost war comrades.

31

As soon as I came out of the expressionless grey building I hailed a cab. The rain had let up, and after the rush hour it wasn't difficult. I told the Pakistani driver my address. I wanted get out there as fast as I had arrived.

The driver asked if I wanted take FDR down. I told him anywhichway he wished would be fine.

I snuggled myself in the seat, let my eyes follow the moving scenery. The cab sped through the street where the high-rise condos towered one next to another. It got to be strange living up there so above everything. On thirtieth floor. On thirty-first floor. Don't they get suicidal fits sometime? Hope they at least make sure not to leave the windows wide open so their cats won't jump off. . . .

All at once I felt invincibly alone.

Kira was always the axis which I orbited around. Since the first day we met. She's selfish, vain, obnoxios, conceited—who doesn't have a trace of all these traits?—but also amusing, amazing, amiable creature. One of a kind.

She was my confidante, more so than I was to her. Any trouble I had I'd tell her, and she'd listen attentively, get me some drink, pat my shoulder and say 'lighen up, girl!'.

At times when I was caught in brooding loneliness, I'd put fins and flares to the story, or entirely make up a problem about boys, so she could show me—only me—the big toothy smile of encouragement.

But now she says she is going away. For a month. Maybe more. But who does she think she's kidding? What happens after that? Does she think she can chain Stephen with a sense of guilt until he finally gives her the ultimatum? Is she that afraid of taking grip on her life? No matter how hard it is?

She well knows going away doesn't lead anywhere. She's giving herself a rain check. The decision got to be made. You could delay once but it has to be done. Nothing in this world settles by itself—except perhaps the world—universe itself. We, the fragments have to find our way around. For both of us, for all of us, the time has passed and time is passing. No turning back, no escape. You know that, Kira!

I wiped my eyes with back of my hand.

". . . . . Miss, are you all right?"

The worrisome eyes peeked at me through the rear view mirror.

"Uh-huh——"

I nodded and gave a swallow.

"——I've lost my kitty."

32

"Are you traveling together?"

The lady at the check-in counter asked.

"No. I'm seeing her off," I said.

"Oh, O.K. . I wanted to make sure."

The lady gave a sincere smile and typed in some information into the computer. While she was at it I admired her fuscia lipstick that went nicely with her silvery hair. Somehow it was very French.

"How many bags are you checking?"

"Two," Rie said and giggled.

She came to New York with only one suitcase, but after a last-minute shopping spree she had to get an extra nylon bag to put all the stuff in. I knew she had to buy a few more things—souvenirs—in the duty-free. It was good Masahiko was coming to the airport.

The airline lady checked Rie's passport. A lot smaller one than the one I (used to)have.

"O.K. . The boarding starts at 10:15 (she circled the time with a green pen), at gate 19. You're all set."

"Thank you," I said, and we went up on the escalator.

The concourse was filled with swarms of people. A lot

of them Japanese. Perhaps they were on the same flight with Rie.

"What shall we do?"I asked Rie.

"Well, let's have my last cup of American coffee."

I stood in the line while Rie looked for a table. Here and there I heard the strayed bits of chat in Japanese. A lot of women and not so many men. They were all around late fifties to early sixties—right about the same age as my parents. Their loudness was rather embarrasing although it made me comfortable, warm. When I closed my eyes, it sounded like I was standing in Ueno Station.

"What's up with your eyes closed?" Rie asked.

"I was remembering how it was in Ueno Station."

"Ueno Station!" she burst into laughter.

"Seems like a long time."

"I bet. Even I haven't been there. Two years? Three years? Since the last time I went to skiing. But God, you haven't been there after the bullet-train started run, have you? It got cleaned up a lot. It's a different world."

"How're things in Ame-Yoko?"

"I don't know really. I suppose you can still get work clothes—overalls and coveralls cheap there But imports? The age of Chanel and Hermes, I don't think many go there. It's too crummy.

"You're probably right," I said.

It's not the kind of place I'd want to go if I lived in Tokyo. Too chaotic. Perhaps.

"Sis, would you mind if I go shop a little while? Will you watch my bag?"

"Sure," I said.

I let my eyes roam around with the crowd, and listened.

All these people—the regiment of suburban housewives I used to despise—began to appear amicable, even charming somewhat. They scurried here to there, considering what to get for their friends and families who waited for their return home. In the end it may not be a bad place—Japan. I may be making it look terrible in my own heart. By trying to hate it, I may be fueling my guts to stick to this place.

I finished my coffee and absorbed the atmosphere.

"Here."

Rie came back and put a little thing in my hand.

A keyholder—said I ♥ New York in the center of an apple shaped metal.

"A present."

"For me? Why?"

"Well, originally I wanted to get you something from the duty-free but they won't hand me goods untill I board the plane. It's silly, isn't it? But I guess otherwise whole New York gonna come here to shop, right? So, this. I love New York, you love New York."

She made a shape of heart with her fingers.

"Thanks."

I smiled and put it in my jeans pocket, then I shyly added,

"I'll miss you."

"I know, me too."

Rie nodded.

The Japanese tourists around us started to make their move toward the gate. The clock on the wall said quater to ten.

"You'd better go now," I said.
"I suppose," Rie said.

"Passengers only.Passengers only."
An airport security, a black girl with a magnificent cornrows, repeated in front of the X-ray machine.
"Got your boarding pass?" she asked Rie.
Rie took it out of her backpack and showed it to her.
"O.K. . I'm going," Rie said.
"Uh-huh." I nodded.
" Thanks for everything. Call me. Write me. I will, too"
"Yeah, say hello to Masahiko."
"I will"
She gave a big smile.
"So long."
"So long."
From behind the glass I followed Rie's back go through the metal detector.
After she picked up her backpack from the X-ray machine she waved. I waved back. I watched her till she disappeared into the curved corridor.
I stood there while other Japanese were being processed one by one. They looked happy. Full of excitement on going home
Suddenly I felt this urge to join them. Join the people who were able to bring others the nice memories of their trip. People who would recollect on and on wistfully about the places they saw, things they did. I bit my lips.
As I walked down the stairs to get outside, the harsh reflection of a car window blinded me for a second.

It seemed to be another bright sunny day, a nice day to sit in a park, to ride a bike. But how many sunny days can you really take? What would Rie say if I called her up from the phonebooth around the corner from her tomorrow? Would she welcome me with a smile?

It's just a thought. But then who knows?